In China with Harpo and Karl

The publication of this book was supported with grants from the National Endowment for the Arts and the Oregon Arts Commission.

Cover art, *Red Dragon,* acrylic and collage, by Debbie Berrow.
Cover design by Carolyn Sawtelle.
Book design by Carolyn Sawtelle and Cheryl McLean.

CALYX Books are distributed to the trade by The Talman Company Inc., 150 Fifth Ave., NY, NY 10011, 212-620-3182. CALYX Books are also available through major library distributors and jobbers and most small press distributors including: Airlift, Bookpeople, Bookslinger, Inland Book Co., Pacific Pipeline, and Small Press Distribution. For personal orders or other information write: CALYX Books, PO Box B, Corvallis, OR 97339, 503-753-9384.

Library of Congress Cataloging-in-Publication Data
James, Sibyl.
    In China with Harpo and Karl / Sibyl James.
        p.   cm.
    ISBN 0-934971-16-1 :(alk.paper): $17.95. — ISBN 0-934971-15-3
(pbk. : alk. paper): $9.95
        1. China—Description and travel—1976—I. Title.
    DS712.J34   1990
    951.05'8' 0207—dc20   90-1974
                                                             CIP

Printed in the U.S.A.

In China with Harpo and Karl

by Sibyl James

CALYX Books
Corvallis, Oregon

ACKNOWLEDGMENTS

The author acknowledges the following publications in which these essays were previously published: "Somewhere in North America" first appeared in *Sun Dog: The Southeast Review*, Fall 1987. "The Word the Men Don't Know" first appeared in a slightly different version under the title "Notes from China" in *The American Voice*, No. 17, Winter 1989. "The Carp's Genes," "Spitting," "*Fu Wu Yuan*," and "China's Chinatown" were published in *Gulf Stream*, No. 2, Spring 1990.

For the people of the PRC,
and the people passing through.

TABLE OF CONTENTS

I
THE MONKEY QUEEN

II
SCHOOL DAYS

III
Harpo and Karl

IV
Between Language and Actual Time

V
THINGS FOREIGN

VI
MODERN FLIGHTS

VII
PARABLES OF THE MIDDLE KINGDOM

PREFACE

Recently I spent a year teaching at a college in Shanghai, People's Republic of China. People often ask me how I managed such an arrangement. The initial step was simple: I wrote the Ministry of Education in Beijing, answering an ad for "foreign experts" that I'd seen in the journal of the Modern Language Association. That step launched me into a year of letters and cables and plans, ending in a cliffhanger wait for the arrival of a visa and plane ticket. (A late-night call from China to some other teachers also waiting for tickets announced that we should go to "United States Airlines." There is only one airline in China—the state-owned CAAC. We decided the Chinese must think our country's skies are equally singular. We called United; we were right.)

I'd always wanted to visit China—always been interested in the country politically. But the costs of traveling there had seemed prohibitive. Now the Chinese government was offering me a free roundtrip, a modest salary, and housing in the old section of Shanghai's Jin Jiang Hotel, where other foreign teachers often lived. When I arrived in Shanghai in late August, the college's official greeters whisked me past customs and the humid night streets to my hotel. There I embarrassed everyone—first, by lying down on both of the room's beds to determine which should be removed, then by ordering a beer in the restaurant. It arrived in a bottle the size of a fifth of wine and no one would help me drink it.

In the States, I write and teach part-time at various colleges, piecing several three-month contracts together over the year to eke out a living. My friend Ed, also a part-timer and also going off to teach in China, noted that for the first time in our lives we were being offered a one-year contract with medical benefits. Actually, I never saw the contract itself until the late spring of my Chinese year, and by the time it appeared I didn't bother to sign it. But I visited the hospital often.

And that is perhaps the heart of the tale. For these pages are the stories and meditations of a resident foreigner, not a tourist—and all the sickness and cures, the struggles and trust that such a status confers.

Sibyl James

POSTSCRIPT

This book presents the China I knew in 1985-86, a China ruptured now by the massive peaceful protests and the government's retaliatory violence in the spring of 1989, the spring, in particular, of Tian'anmen Square. In Seattle I followed that struggle like an addict, tuning in to every broadcast on National Public Radio, listening to its reruns while stuck in traffic on the way to class, scavenging the ferry that I rode from my peninsula cabin for newspapers—more headlines, more photos, more news. My great fear, my great complaint while I lived in China had always been that the new economic ventures meant only the freedom to buy things, a materialist freedom I valued far less than personal ones—like the freedom to travel, to say and write what one wished, to choose the job one wanted even if that choice meant (as mine always had) that the rewards were something other than financial. I felt that the students and workers were demonstrating for the very rights I'd thought the Chinese ought to fight for—not the right to a capitalist economy but the right to an economy and society free of exploitation and corruption, a society of personal freedom and justice. I wanted to be with them so badly I nearly walked out on my Seattle teaching job and took the next plane. At first the news was heady, impossibly jubilant; it seemed as if that nagging sense I'd learned in China, that sense that something could always go wrong, was itself wrong this time. It seemed as if the students and the others who had joined them would win. I was on the edge of tears, reading about Zhao Zi Yang cautioning the students to be prudent, saying of the leaders, "We're old, we don't care anymore"—reading about the Chinese climbing onto trucks packed with the People's Liberation Army, saying, "Don't do this, you're the people's army." Only in China, I said, could government leaders suddenly speak such honest truths; only in China did they name the army the people's. And then it was the fourth of June. And the people's army was not theirs.

Tonight, I'm sitting in Tunisia, where I teach now, watching a documentary of China on the French television channel. Like this book, it was created before Tian'anmen, but the images of Tian'anmen bracket its beginning—a student standing before the tanks. Even the title, from the book by Alain Peyrefitte, has taken on ironic overtones: *Quand la Chine s'eveillera*—When China will awaken. But after that beginning image, Peyrefitte's earlier China and mine return: Here's Shanghai, Longhua Temple with its monks, the pedestrian bridge over busy Nanjing Lu, the bicycles, the street markets with fish swimming in basins and plucked chickens hanging from a hook, old men in baggy shorts doing *Tai Ji* beside old women with bobby pins pulling back their short grey hair. Here are my favorite barge-like boats plying the murky waters, the tea fields of Hangzhou, the silk factory I never got around to visiting, a formal garden (could it be The Master of the Nets where my friend Suzanne and I once sat for hours over tea?). Here are rag mops propped against the wall in some narrow street, a hospital with doctors demonstrating acupuncture and their incredible techniques of restorative surgery on a hand lost in some third-world machine. Interspersed is footage from pre-liberation China, detailing the poverty and hardship of the past versus what seems riches now in living color. How clean it all seems on TV, how less chaotic! The sun is shining on Tian'anmen with the huge portrait of Mao hanging before the Forbidden City, his mausoleum, the museums, and the Great Hall of the People—all of it seeming far more vast in this camera shot than in my memory where it sits more intimately laid out, more accessible. In my memory, like this long sunny camera shot, there is no bloodshed. That violence is a frame added later, that at first in June 1989 had seemed to me to betray and render senseless everything I'd written about China, every kind word and complaint, the humor that I'd couched my tale in and had needed to survive my Chinese year. Yet I knew the seeds of everything that happened in the spring of 1989 had been there all along.

There is a Chinese saying that goes something like this: "You don't make the grass grow faster by pulling it." Like the students and workers in Tian'anmen I am a puller and hate the times we're forced to lie low and wait. But I believe the grass keeps growing. On the documentary now, a soundtrack of Chinese pop lyrics over a disco beat begins, while people pass, hauling high-piled carts, carrying heavy loads on shoulder poles, and two girls walk away together under umbrellas into the misty rain. It's suddenly the end of the program, of what the French call an "emission," like a signal cast out into space. Just enough to make me homesick for that country where so much grass waits to be pulled.

Sibyl James
Tunis, Fall 1989

I

The Monkey Queen

Roach Pills

My hotel's famous in Shanghai. My friends from home can send me letters with only the name, Jin Jiang Hotel, and in a city of six million, their news will find me.

The Jin Jiang is really a complex of buildings, including shops, a beauty salon, restaurants, even a post office and tele-type. It's also a complex of hotels: two tall ones, reminiscent of Chicago architecture from the 1930s, and a shorter 1950s box, then a shabby line of what were once row houses, converted now to rooms where long-term, low-rent visitors like myself are housed. I crank my third-story window open onto views of the green lawn that fronts one of the grander buildings, with a circle drive where limousines sometimes wait for visiting diplomats, the drivers shining the hoods with feather dusters they store in the space below the car's rear window. Years ago, Zhou En Lai opened China to Nixon in the Jin Jiang.

But the high concrete walls around this square-block compound keep it closed to locals. The same walls line streets where the foreigners once lived in mansions, in the days when foreigners ruled sections of the city, before the Long March and Liberation. The bikes in the old driveways and the laundry hanging on poles from mansion windows testify that crowds of the country's families live there now. But the Chinese doormen close the Jin Jiang's gates on other Chinese. If my Shanghai friends come to visit, they must sign in with their names and mine—something they rarely wish to do—or I must meet them at the gate and escort them in. Chinese with connections seem to pass without a foreigner, as do the Chinese from Hong Kong. Try not to dress local, we tell our friends; try to look like you're from Hong Kong. Useless advice. No one, not even we foreigners, can dress as fashionably as Hong Kong Chinese. We give up, find ways to work around the walls, to accommodate the rules.

But never to accommodate the roaches, the only local visitors that slip past, or maybe camped here long before the walls went up around them. The Jin Jiang's more famous in the China guidebooks for its roaches than its diplomats. Perhaps there's some connection. I think of those traps they sell in the States called roach hotels, the commercial that says the roaches check in and don't check out. Perhaps the Jin Jiang's one large trap, keeping the rest of the city roach-free.

The war begins crudely at first, with shoes for weapons, until we comprehend the numbers ranged against us. Then my friend Peggy, who has also recently arrived from the States, and is also plagued by roaches, remembers boric acid, that old home remedy. And it's not even hard to find in the shops, only difficult to say in Chinese; I ask a friend to write the characters on a slip of paper. I sprinkle the white powder in the corners, every drawer, the medicine chest. Immune to Western poisons, the roaches walk blatantly across my desk. Every day, I find one sitting on the bristles of my toothbrush. I wrap the brush in toilet paper, bag up other favorite targets, learn the rules of the occupying forces.

One day, at school, Professor Wang, a distinguished member of the faculty, asks how I find the Jin Jiang, am I comfortable there? Everyone knows it's a famous hotel and everyone would want the best for the foreign expert. I confess about the roaches. He laughs, delighted, I think, to hear the truth, and to find how much we share besides our intellectual concerns, something that unites us beyond separate cultures, this common hunger for the dignity of mornings without roaches.

A week later, someone at the school brings me a small package from Professor Wang. Inside, I find brown tablets. Roach pills, says the messenger. Put them where the roaches walk. I do. And the pills stay there, uneaten all year. I never see another roach.

Still, I keep my bread inside a closed tin pot, wrap my cereal box in a plastic bag—some old Chinese habit of maintaining walls.

BLESSINGS ON THE BRITISH CONSUL

I've settled in. I've cleaned my room, swept it with a reed broom, the purple berries still clinging to the dried stems. I've scrubbed the wood floor with its years of caked red wax, down on my hands and knees one humid night in my bikini, hoping the school's official greeter wouldn't turn up in the midst of my red-smudged sweat to introduce me to some newly arrived foreign guest.

One bulb glows yellow from the high ceiling and lights the faded blue and white print walls, the paper brown-stained near the turquoise metal unit that blows heat or chills, depending on the brand of water that's piped through it. I've hung a five-foot map of China and a big red flag above my single bed, stripped the drapes from the windows, rolled up the carpet alive with whatever breeds in centuries of ground-in dust, lugged it into the hall. I like the room's spare barren look, with only my small straw mat on the floor, the tall windows that open on metal cranks. I would break their frosted panes to get them replaced with clear glass, but I heard that another hotel resident tried that last year and simply had to live the winter out with taped cracks.

But this is August, not December, and the heat hangs, heavy as a padded Chinese quilt. The water that the thermoses keep hot for tea does nothing for my constant thirst. The thin sweet orange drink sold in shops without refrigeration works no better. The night's thirst stretches out, more blackly oppressive than its heat. I can't work—roam the evening streets to keep my mind off dreams of lemonade, Westinghouse cold. Most Chinese live without refrigerators. I wonder do they thirst like this, or is the love of liquid ice a foreign habit? I find myself standing outside a shop's windows, staring at the display: one refrigerator, the door open, food cartons and bottles on the immaculate shelves. I remember life was like that once, luxuries so easily familiar, so taken for granted. I stand a long time, transfixed, like a tourist at the emperor's palace.

Back in my room I write letters, forgetting to mention the exotic sights of China, reminiscing about refrigeration. Later in the week, the foreigners gather for a party. I meet some teachers from England who live in my hotel. They've been here longer; they have connections with the British Consul who's loaned one of them a small icebox the size of a television set. But just this week their school has placed refrigerators in every teacher's room. The Consul's appliance now sits unplugged in a closet, consuming precious storage space. I feel like a pilgrim about to drink the healing waters of Our Lady of Lourdes. Yes, the British promise, smiling, you can pick the icebox up tomorrow.

I'm a willing colonist. I'll never dump tea in the Shanghai harbor, never rebel. Each time I open the icebox door, I know some things are more important to rule than the waves. The cap pops off the bottle like a cannon hailing Britannia; the ice against the cold glass chants "God Save the Queen."

Neighborly Noise

It's about 10:30 p.m. and I'm feeling a need for the sounds of home. From the giant cardboard box that doubles as my second suitcase, I unearth my cheap tape recorder and a cassette by Dire Straits. The room has just begun to rattle to the beat of foreign decadence when somebody knocks on my door. It's a tiny wisp of a young Scottish woman, Shirley, my new neighbor, who covers her mouth when she whispers, "Oh, I've been ill—and the plane and the long flight—and just arrived," and flutters and could be blown away by easy listening, certainly by Dire Straits. "Of course," I say. "I'll turn it down."

Next week, the Hong Kong men move in across the hall, construction workers on the nearby joint-venture hotel. Maybe five, maybe ten of them in one room—I'm never sure. They leave their door open, hang out smoking in the hall. They play Chinese checkers through the night, slapping the huge counters on the table. They spit; they talk a lot. It is impossible to do either of these things quietly in Chinese.

Shirley flutters up and down the hall, rapping on their door—"Excuse me, the talk, the checkers on the table." I wonder how she tolerates the service people, who walk in at any time with glasses, water, or just to check what's going on. Distractedly, she always hangs the "Don't Disturb" sign wrong side out on her door; it reads "Please Make Up This Room Right Now." One day she locks herself inside the bathroom inside her own locked room and the second lock jams and she's stuck until the service people happen by. Soon after that, she moves.

And Ruth moves in, from Ireland. She doesn't seem to mind Dire Straits. Neither of us likes the pre-dawn spitter who passes regularly beneath our windows. Or the pile drivers down the street. Or the rats that Brian's caught below us in his room. One night, lying in bed, I hear shrieks, then the voice of the hotel attendant, then Irish anger. I understand the rats have made it to our floor.

But this could happen also in New York. It's the sound of the checkers that stays foreign and the seven-toned song of Cantonese. Some days I back Ruth up when she complains to management and a useless sign gets posted on the Hong Kong door, big Chinese characters invoking silence. Mostly, I don't care. I assume the stutter of my old Smith Corona portable is enough revenge. On hung-over Sundays—with the pile drivers tuning up, the jackhammers biting into the shop below me, and someone remodeling the wall behind my bed—I think OK, it's China, better laugh, there's no place to escape.

One night I wake to doors slamming over and over and the high volume horror sounds of Michael Jackson's "Thriller." I remember when I went to bed the Hong Kong boys were slapping down the checkers, but the bangs I hear now come from booted feet. I crack my door and find Ruth in the hall, stomping and slamming—her eyes shut, lips curled in a bliss of vengeance. Carefully, I close the door.

Somehow I sleep until the spitter crows.

IN MY FIVE-YEAR PLAN
THERE'LL BE NO PIGEONS

I'm afraid of birds. I like to watch them at binocular distance but no closer. In the States I never eat at those summer sidewalk tables, set up outside the fashionable restaurants, with someone feeding French bread crumbs to a sparrow and pigeons ambling between the diners' legs. My hatred begins with pigeons and generalizes from there to everything feathered, even the peacock tails of art deco earrings.

One of the first things I notice about China, one of the first things I love, is the near absence of pigeons. Infrequently, a few fly overhead; they never land. Perhaps it is the same small flock passing. Sometimes I see a pair in a cage outside a home; sometimes a boy walks by with one clutched tightly in his hand, presumably the night's dinner. I never see a pigeon on the street. Possibly they're smarter than I think and understand that solid Shanghai traffic and twelve million feet leave no safe space for pigeon landings.

Maybe their genes carry some handed-down memory of the days just after Liberation, when Mao declared war on the four pests: rats, lice, flies, and starlings. To eliminate the starlings, all the Chinese gathered outside on a designated day, shouting, beating drums and pots and pans, beating anything to scare the starlings, to keep them circling in the air until they dropped from exhaustion and were killed. Of course, what worked for the starlings also killed the other birds, no way to discriminate, to beat a special rhythm deadly only to the pest.

I don't think this story is apocryphal. I've seen the Chinese on campaigns. I've read about the men who kept trying to build a military installation in an unlikely, impossible spot, simply because their general's pencil had made a stray mark there on a map, and they thought he meant it. I can happily verify the lack of birds.

Besides, the Chinese like lists. Paul, a Canadian teacher, tells me of an article he read, about how everything in China has always been enumerated: the ten do's and don'ts of Confucianism, the four modernizations, the five-year plans, the four pests. That, we agree, is what our students want—a list of truths to memorize. How easy to be clear then. And what does it matter if some unintended casualties attend the carrying out of lists, if the pigeons go down with the starlings? But what about the herons and the hummingbirds? Even a hater of birds has hierarchies of tolerance. To carry out a list is simple, but to compose one? To determine its criteria? Lists in the Cultural Revolution shifted daily, and ten years later, people can still doubt which one they're on.

The birds are coming slowly back. I read in the *China Daily* about a man who received an award for saving some endangered ducks. I read in the *San Francisco Chronicle*, in Herb Caen's column, that some Chinese in Beijing would like a flock of pigeons "to add grace to Tian'anmen Square." San Francisco's a sister city to Beijing, and Caen proposes a sisterly gesture, happy to ship off every feather.

Like the Chinese, I make lists, enjoy crossing things off as they're finished. At the top of my list of pests, I put the pigeons—flying rats that carry lice, their coos more annoying than a bluefly's small buzz. I discriminate, leaving the countryside out of my program, knowing no bird's as urban as a pigeon. In my five-year plan, I designate one day when diners in their silks and suits will stand up at sidewalk cafes, rapping their forks against their China plates, rubbing fingers on their crystal glasses till the rims wail.

11

HAIRCUT

Hairdressers intimidate me. I feel insecure with my hair wet and combed back for the cut, my face too visible, exposed. It becomes the face of my mother, and I judge it with the same words she has used about herself for years. Unstylish, raw-boned. Whether these are true perceptions doesn't matter. This is how we feel.

I should abandon this attitude in China, where my face charms crowds if only by its difference, and fashion is a concept so newly allowed that anything can wear its name. Here, the fashion names for haircuts sound like movements in *Tai Ji*: "flapping wing," "explosion," "one-side parting style."

In the *China Daily*, I read about Zhou Yunyao, a peasant who came to Shanghai thirty years ago and apprenticed in a hair salon. He mopped the floors, washed towels, and heated water. He observed. But the Cultural Revolution called hairdressing bourgeois and shut the shop down.

Now he thrives, a man engrossed by his trade. At foreign films he ignores the plots, fascinated only by the hairstyles. He guarantees his clients' satisfaction, changed one young woman's hair three times before she left him, smiling.

Zhou's guarantee would do me no good. I'm more meek in hair salons than in a doctor's office. I try to name my wishes indirectly, some wistful comment dropped about how much

12

I love long curls. And smile always at the finish, smile through paying up and out the door to find the nearest bathroom, start over with my own comb.

Before I came to China, I had nearly all my hair cut off, thinking this would make life simpler. A mistake. Long hair simply grows; short hair needs the scissors often. Zhou's shop is out of the question—no way to find it. No number listed in the *China Daily*, and I've never seen a phone directory in Shanghai. So I try the shop at my hotel, reassuring with its Western decor, its cutters in white coats lounging in idle chairs. I come casually dressed—shorts and a t-shirt—forgetting the salon serves tourists from the hotel's grander rooms, while I live in its slum bowels. The man in charge, clearly the expert stylist, waves me off on some young girl. I think "apprentice." Perhaps she mops the floor, as Zhou once did, and watches, learning her trade between the wet towels. She sets me in a chair, pours cream in my dry hair, and lathers it into bubbles. This, I learn, is typical in China. With every cut you get a head massage. Today, it seems a debatable bonus. Her nails are long as a Mandarin's, carving my skull like jade.

A wash. And now the cut. My usual insecurities are overlaid with fear and the lack of a language I can trust. She drives the big comb deep into my head and grabs a random handful, chops it just as randomly, and moves on to the next. The expert goes on lounging in his chair beside the other young girls, and all of them chat gleefully with mine in Shanghai dialect, a language where I know only the words for "help me" and lack the nerve to say them now.

My mother's face stares at me from the mirror. It fakes a smile.

BUSING

First, be short. Or stand beneath an open skylight in the bus roof. Be thin. Be very thin. To get on or off be Kung Fu elbows and not sorry.

In China, nothing comes more often than a bus. It doesn't matter. Crowd panic will jam the first one, people on the street pushing the last immobilized crush of bodies forward till the folding doors can shut around them, like sitting on a stuffed suitcase to snap the latch.

Crammed between men's groins, I'm glad the country isn't sexual yet. When the young boys affecting Western punk haircuts and cigarettes grow up, I'll spend the money for a cab. Now I only drape my shopping bags around my waist like bulky armor.

In the night street, buses drive with only parking lights, sometimes flash their headlights like a warning horn. Once I read the Chinese drove like this because they thought it saved electrical power. Ask my friend Professor Wang, he calls it poor management. Ask me, I call it macho, like the Mexican drivers who brag of navigating the mountains between Oaxaca and San Cristóbal in the dark.

At every stoplight the driver turns the engine off. Maybe thinks it saves gas. Maybe not. Maybe shuts down automatic as the country's natural rhythm, like a shop clerk or a waiter shuts down deader than idle, unless forced.

The stops where you can get off don't come often. Miss yours, walk a mile back. Name your street, the ticketer will take your money, doors will close and stay closed till the other side of town. Or the ticketer won't take your money, will swear this bus you took there last week doesn't make that stop, will argue helpfully for miles until you get off where you wanted with a free ride.

I name the wrong stop, and an old woman pokes me in the chest, repeatedly, makes elaborate pantomines that mean "I'll lead, you follow." When the doors open, she grips my arm down the street at a run, and parks me at the right stop. This is known as friendly.

Friendly is also the occasional seat given up with much polite fuss to the foreigner. More friendly is the woman who takes a live chicken from a seatless man and holds it out the window.

The ticketer always has a seat and a small red flag with five stars, unfurled at stops. For days, I admired the country's honesty. Easy not to hand your money over in those crowds. I forgot how much the Chinese learn to memorize in school. The ticketer knows every face that's paid and every one that hasn't.

Last week at Hong Kou Park, I saw a bonsai exhibition—stalls and stalls of tiny trees bent into shapes the Chinese find pleasing, a sort of stay against the chaos of the natural. Suddenly I understood the secret of buses. My bones leaned together, my chest concaved. I found a space that fit me when the doors shut.

THE BANK

The Bank: because in Shanghai there really is just one that counts—the Bank of China on the waterfront, part of the line of marble and neo-classic grandeur surviving from the days of the British and French. And it is still the place where foreigners deal, threading their way through constant reconstruction projects, up the broad steps where marble glimmers through the sawdust.

My first trip to the bank begins at 1:45 and ends three hours later. A long bus ride, then a short walk from the last stop. Inside, the bank's airy and high-ceilinged as a cathedral, but busy as a bus station, with crowds waiting to receive various documents from the maze of different work stations ranged along two lengthy counters. Behind the counters, and placed perpendicular to them, stand rows of long tables. These tables are strewn with the tea cups of gossiping employees and tiny onion-slender slips of Chinese paper in bundles clipped together by dressmakers' straight pins. Any transaction involves a confusing shuffle back and forth among these various stations.

Today I want to trade some *renminbi*, what I call "people's money," for FEC, the Foreign Exchange Currency that buys goods like imported cigarettes and wine. First I must have signed forms from my school, proving that I'm allowed to do

16

this. Then, I hand over my money and get nothing back except a scrap of paper with a number. The receipt—done in triplicate with separate carbons that have to be carefully replaced inside the pad each time—is straight-pinned, then housed in an oval plastic box which is fired down the counter in a groove, like kids racing slot-cars. The box is the only thing that moves fast. Luckily, the center of the bank is lined with large brown imitation leather couches.

I wander between stations, trading forms and numbers. Finally, I join the last "line," really a group of people in mixed stages of patient humor and frustration, milling around the counter. We watch employees pick up slips of paper, count out money in various local and foreign denominations, then clip it all together and lob it, in an underhanded softball swing, down the table where someone counts again and then repeats the toss. This is the most important table and the one that takes the longest. Invariably some essential person in the counting line-up decides to take a bathroom break or heat more water for fresh tea, and strolls off, soap and towel and cup in hand, just as your toss reaches that station.

And finally there's the woman with the microphone who calls the numbers off to signify it's time, your money's here. She does this first in Shanghai dialect, which most foreigners can't understand. So we stand around with our numbers face up on the counter, hoping to catch her eye. But so often we catch only her back, as she sits facing her coworkers in an endless chat. Once, my Australian friend Antoinette, seeing a packet of money with her number sitting by the microphone, leaned over the counter and held her own scrap of number near the woman's head, precisely where eye level would be, if she ever turned her eyes back to the waiting crowd. Antoinette held her number there a long time till the laughter of coworkers did the job.

We learn quickly that a trip to the bank requires a trip to the bar at the next-door Peace Hotel immediately afterwards. We share our stories: the day the school was out of FEC but didn't tell me, sent me off anyway with the forms, leaving it to the bank employees to drop the bomb. The day Paul watched a worker feed a stack of bills into a counting machine, with the total coming up different each time—98, 87, 92, 100—ah, the total he wanted. And so that count must be correct, no need to check it. He smiled and wrapped a rubberband around the stack. Or the stifling day everybody was too busy with fans to bother working, till I pulled my camera out to snap the lack of action.

We leave half our money at the bar, but we leave happy. At the street stands, we stop for fried bread, watch it make its way from rolled dough to our mouths through an assembly line of hands, and think how much we love this rhythm of collective effort, love it everywhere except the place it always breaks down, paydays at the bank.

THE OPERA'S RISING STAR

I don't like opera in the West: too mink-stoled, too stout-chested, too often Wagnerian. But I'll stay East forever if I can star in Chinese opera, let the drums and clashing gongs announce my entrances, their beat dramatic as my feelings. I'll drop my arms and let my long silk sleeves unfurl until they trail past hands and hit the floor, a gesture signifying sudden anger, ecstasy, or desolation. I'll call them back in graceful lifts, until they pleat my wrist, each fold a new decision laid out in my song, another layer of plot.

I spend hours in the opera store, with its glass cases of patterned robes, big rhinestone pins, and earrings like chandeliers. Fake jewels drip from the wires on headdresses, a trembling sparkle in the spotlights. All the boots have soles built up six inches, reminding us how passion's taller on the stage. The grandest boots wear dragon faces.

My favorite clothes belong to male roles and to the *hua dan*, the feistier heroines who flash across the stage in baggy silk trousers cuffed at each ankle like harem pants. But nothing's harem-like about their characters. Even their bodies talk back, making long, arrogant strides or leaping in acrobatic battles, quick heels kicking sword after enemy sword into the air. The gentler heroines take small bound steps and droop, sing-

19

ing as plaintively as the strings of the *erhu* that accompanies them, keeping their red-lipsticked mouths in a tight bow.

Everything's grandly artificial. Everything's been stylized, so a circle of steps around the stage becomes a journey, a finger crooked this way means joy, every move perfected for years. And still, a people's art, born in the streets, a kind of heroic vaudeville going on then for hours, painted faces under the gas lamps. Old people know the songs by heart, gather some days in the corner of a park to sing. The audience for opera is mostly old; young people prefer movies and the coffee shops, the places that play tapes of Hong Kong disco.

I don't like disco, but I love the Rolling Stones, camped out all night for tickets once in Seattle to watch Mick Jagger's moves on stage. The opera stars have moves that rival Jagger's. I remember the audience one evening in a fit of the applause that's rare in China, clapping while a son and his mother sang their way from both ends of the long stage, arms out, shuddering forward on their knees till they embraced in the melodramatic middle. I swear that my favorite opera star, Sun Wu Kong—the Monkey King—is the Chinese prototype for Jagger. He's an acrobat, juggling swords against his long pole, tossing one up to catch it in a scabbard. He pulls a few hairs from his arm, blows them into extra monkeys. He never kills his enemies; he wins by style and clever tricks. Standing on one foot, he blinks cool lashes, dusted with gold glitter.

The stories of the Monkey King are the finest that the country has invented. Over and over he journeys off to fetch the sacred scriptures with his crew of companions—one silent and stoic; one a sidekick in the guise of a pig, always after food and women, always made a butt of, the homelier side of humanity; and the last, a monk, naive and helpless, constantly in some fix. Sun Wu Kong's a rebel, but the gods who govern him are rebels too, like Greek ones, loving to play tricks, benevolent and firm at once. Sometimes a female intercessor that my friend Paul calls the Virgin Mary appears in the skies at crucial moments—to mediate between the Monkey King and whatever gods or villains he's at odds with, to help him out of a jam.

I've loved the Monkey King since I first saw him in his opera battle with the white snake woman—played, of course, by a *hua dan*. I got the opera's point, even though my Chinese friend translated only obvious moments. When a man wearing a beak and a red rooster's comb ran about the stage, she turned to me and whispered importantly, "a chicken!"

I'm Western. I love the sound of clapping hands and know I won't get that in China, where the audience is apt to talk throughout performances and walk out as the last song's ending, with the slides of written characters that help the people understand the words still flashing on the wall. Applause is not a Chinese habit. But once, the crowd left their seats and rushed forward while the heroine was singing the story's dénouement. What's happening, I asked my friend. She's young, he said, and very good. They want to get a closer look at this new star.

Sometimes I crank my hotel window open on the night, find one star burning always in the same place, so big and bright it seems a planet, a whole world shining, so different from my own. I call it "Monkey Queen." I dream we rise together, happy, when the houselights of the sky dim, kicking up our feet in baggy silk, sure that silence is the way the universe applauds.

CHINA RECONSTRUCTS

Everyone must get off the bus or truck at the launching ramp and wait, then get back on to board the ferry, more like a large amphibious landing craft, with the tailgates hoisted at either end, and the brown Yangtse pouring through the grating. Midway across the river, a string of wooden barges curves by, filled with tractors that could be Dust Bowl exhibits, only they're new. This is China reconstructing.

Bamboo scaffolding: the weave of it is finer than the building going up behind. Nothing will happen for weeks and then a midnight wave of noise and in the morning the homes are there, the concrete prefab softened by balconies of laundry and potted plants. China reconstructs.

The hotel is half erected, half torn down, gangplanks for walks and the pipes outside, exposed and steaming. It could be any building. It could be the institute where I teach, celebrating its twenty-fifth anniversary with two students reciting "Snow White" and the Central Committee men making speeches lost in the dull roar of audience gossip. Every speech lists successes. Every speech names shortcomings at the end and hopes it hasn't wasted your time. Everyone makes a five-year plan.

Technology is in this, and everyone's in love with that.

The man who drove a water buffalo now drives my taxi, drives a hot jazz drummer's solo on the horn, the headlights flashing like a high-hat cymbal crash. He keeps the plastic wrapping on the seats, signs three sets of forms for every fare.

Easy to understand the way the photocopier becomes a shrine, nirvana under its green velvet cover. Washing my clothes at the sink, I dream I find a coin Whirlpool in the hotel lobby, watch it spinning like a waltz.

China Reconstructs. It's the name of a magazine I never read, only see the reality of its pages turning on the roads torn up for miles, the dust more steady than the spades of the three men digging, nobody paid to hold a flag.

Tones mean everything in this language. There are tones for "China Reconstructs," but only two count. The first is the one I use most often, dripping irony around the dust and the bodies sprawled in two hours of *xiuxi*—a "little rest"—each noon.

In the second, my throat is full of pasts that move behind the drivers shining their cabs and the young girls in their red high-heeled boots. The tones are men with beards and wide cheekbones and old, old women in high collars, on a long march.

SPITTING

It's the first rhythm of China, a percussion like the gongs of Beijing Opera, only less dramatic. You can hear it priming like an old pump in the chest or a motor revving till the rust turns juicy, bubbles up and out.

Men spit. Women spit less often. I've never seen a child spit, but it could be something they grow up to, like high heels and sex. I picture a boy scraping his three short chin hairs in his first shave. Afterwards, his father takes him outdoors, arm across the shoulders, men together. They clear their throats. They have their first spit.

Outside every cheap hotel in Mexico lives a rooster. Outside every Chinese window lives a spitter. At six, he hawks the sun up, plants it for me in the street.

I wouldn't look, but somehow I have to, the way a crowd gathers around a fatal accident. Even blind, the sound would still be graphic, a long dry heave, sometimes in series, like an endless morning-after.

I read the *China Daily*. It tells me there are fines for spitting. But the traffic cop spits, and the People's Liberation Army in their green caps. I imagine a citizen's arrest. The thought of all the forms I'd have to fill out stops me. The thought of someone asking for the evidence.

Good days the air is dust; bad days it's soot. I smoke a pack a day in self-defense. Last night I lay in bed and felt the oily bubble starting in my chest. I begin to think it's something to accept, gracefully, like the second line starting under my chin. In the dark I try a few half-silent crows. I wait for six a.m.

Fu Wu Yuan

u wu yuan—the name for the service people in hotels. In humor or exasperation, we shorten it to "the *fu*." Affectionately, we say "my *fu*." They wear black trousers, white shirts, mostly with the tails out or spruced up with a black string tie. Male or female, they have jobs that intersect somewhere between guard dog and maid.

Paranoid days, we think they're paid to watch us, and they probably are, but bumble about it in the most obvious ways. Midnight, when I've thrown a party, one *fu* barges in with the lame excuse that he wants to change the sheets. But my Chinese guests have all gone home already, and the late night squalor of some foreigners is nothing new for his report. Still the *fus* try. Like the night we played cards with Martin and David, two English economists teaching in Shanghai. The game was in Martin's hotel room, and David went downstairs for another bottle of brandy just before the bar closed. The *fu* showed up soon after, with Martin's laundry.

Yes, living in a hotel provides a sort of luxury. The *fus* make the bed as expertly as army privates, and somehow manage every time to knock down the Chinese flag I've hung above it, one scrambling up to repin it, the other in dismay because she's noticed that I've noticed that he's climbing on my blankets in his shoes.

I'm dismayed like her when they catch me cleaning up my room, because, of course, they've come in every day and supposedly cleaned the place. Eventually, I learn to live in what I would otherwise call dirt. Once, the radiator in my bath explodes; this is the only time in one year that the bathroom floor gets mopped by *fus*. They do it with a towel that will reappear next week beside my sink, blackened beyond any wash. I learn to hide towels in my cabinet. Otherwise, they disappear by nine and new ones don't return till two, till after the *fus* have had their noodles and a little rest.

Because the Chinese sometimes sleep on straw mats, the *fus* won't step on the one I use as a rug. They walk carefully around it when they bring my mail. Some mornings are big polishing days; one *fu* guides the machine, leaving chunks of red wax behind on the floor. My feet and the soles of my shoes become the same red.

The *fus* are always trying to learn English, and I am always trying to speak Chinese. The first week, I need toilet paper, but the *fu* can't understand the Chinese phrase I give him, and I refuse to take him to my room to show him, insisting on my language skills. Later, I learn the word is not a compound of the sounds for toilet and paper, but something totally different with its roots in health and sanitation.

When my favorite *fu* loses the English words, she improvises. One day, she enters, says "I want to make a copy..." and not having the name, she walks to my closet, opens it, and reaches confidently for the exact spot where my Mexican *rebozo* hangs. "Shawl," I say, wondering how many times she's tried it on, hoping some morning to surprise the lot of them, male and female, waltzing around the room in my Western skirts and high heels. Before she leaves, she pauses at the door, announces, "I'm twenty-nine, I'm married." The two first bits of information the Chinese always want to know.

My first morning in China, I found a comb and brush with seven years of grease waiting on my sink. I hid them under the bed. Next morning, they were on the sink again. This became a game. Under the bed, back on the sink. Finally, I slipped them under the dust ruffle of some overstuffed chair in the hall. Weeks later, I checked and they were gone.

The night *fu* sleeps in the hall on a temporary cot, his pants tossed over the end, the mosquito coil smouldering. He turns the lights off early; my high heels count out the three flights of concrete in the dark and never wake him.

Or perhaps he's sly as I am. Seven a.m., weekend or not, the *fus* slam through the double doors of my room with a fresh thermos of hot water. I keep the sheet up, keep my eyes closed, feigning sleep. But one of them bangs in and then tiptoes, closes the latch gently. I never learn which one because I have to keep pretending.

The *fus* draw lines as strictly as union members. Once, I borrowed a small refrigerator from another building in the hotel's compound. Those *fus* carried it to my building's entry, left it for my own to help me up the stairs. Within a building, there are hierarchies. The lowest clean the toilet; the highest get the night shift, which means bringing in fresh glasses and sleeping in the hall. My night *fu*'s handsome and a bit evasive. My weekend *fu* is motherly, telling me my plants die because I don't water them enough. The *fus* have balconies full of plants that foreigners have abandoned or half killed. It's good to have a Chinese mother, good to get to know your *fus*, to bribe them with the stamps from foreign letters. At Christmas, I buy a fruitcake, give it to the *fu* on duty, asking him to feed the rest. The next day, my motherly *fu* comes in, wondering where's the present I promised. Apparently, the first one's made off with the whole cake. Nothing to do but go back to the store.

When I travel, the *fus*, of course, always know. There I am in the hall with my red bag; there's the bed for days unslept in. I never tell them what day I'll be back. They have the keys to my room and usually enter while they're still knocking, so hiding my return dates is my only semblance of control. And yet, how strangely fine it is each time the train pulls in, the fight with buses and cabs is over, and I drag back, my bag full of filthy laundry, my own skin longing for the room's erratic shower—and my *fu*s leap up, surprised, from the big chairs in the hall. "*Ni hao*," hello, you're home.

II

School Days

SCHOOL DAYS

Welcoming the Foreign Expert: The old school car arrives to fetch me from my hotel, makes the long drive through the dusty streets of Shanghai to the dustier outskirts where my school sits beside an unpaved road alive with trucks and horns and the cackling of chickens in the market ranged along its sides. Later, when I have to fight the crowds to ride a public bus for more than an hour to reach this same spot, I will appreciate the specialness of this morning's private lift. Later, when I learn that the school's driver is king, that the car's accessibility depends upon his whims, I will appreciate this day's ride even more. But now I am ignorant of all this and simply take the ride as normal hospitality accorded to the foreign guest.

My school, the Shanghai Institute of Foreign Trade, is a four-year college, but looks more like a gathering of high school buildings. Tired flowers and a few bushes of lush blossoming color straggle across the mostly grassless grounds. There are two classroom buildings, a dining hall that doubles as a dance hall and center for big meetings, what passes for a library with an indecipherably chaotic filing system, an office building with a clinic attached, and two dorms, one for students crowded six to a room, one for the slightly less cramped Chinese faculty. Like most of China, everything's concrete, everything's rundown, and everything is under haphazard reconstruction.

A welcoming party of men, in baggy black pants and white short-sleeved shirts with the tails out, herds me around the school. They're smilingly polite, calling me doctor over and over. I'm the first of their foreign experts to wear such a title, and I wonder what they make of how incongruously I fill the image—tapping after them in my high-heeled open sandals, with my toes painted alternately green and blue. By mid-winter I'll be known as Dr. No, the one who always refuses to do what she's told. I'll be known as the table pounder. I will say I'm akin to Nikita Khrushchev. But this is sunny August, and though they probably know what bureaucratic frustrations I'll encounter, I don't yet. Instead, I'm practicing the art of tactful answers to their questions—"Do you think our river's dirty? Do you like the way the women in Shanghai dress?" I learn to answer sideways as they do. Not lies exactly, but not exactly whole truths. I'm learning to be polite and patient and still firm. I'm learning to ask now for what I'll need in three weeks, and get in three months. I'm learning that when these Chinese hosts say "I return in a jiffy," they'll leave me waiting for two hours in my concrete office, with the plastic dull red chairs, the thermos of hot water and the enamel basin, the toilet down the hall that never flushes and the bathroom light that will stay burned out for a year. I'm learning the first of many contradictions.

When the afternoon turns into rain, the school's driver has turned back into king and vanished. A woman teacher washes her rubber boots carefully before presuming to loan them to the foreign expert, but on the school bus no one speaks to me throughout the long ride home.

Lunch: Classes haven't begun yet for the term, but Suzanne—a teacher from Australia—and I have come to school on business and decide to stay for lunch. Once the term begins, the foreign teachers will turn down the offer of a separate foreign dining hall and won't spend much time in the faculty one either. Instead, we'll eat fruit in the relative peace of our offices, or patronize the student dining hall with its long loud tables, where our otherwise shy and polite students jostle and cut ahead of us in line. We'll trade our money for a confusing stack of multicolored plastic tickets, hand these to the women doling rice, tired vegetables, and meat into our white and red enamel school bowls. On the best days, they'll serve *jiaozi*, hot steamed dumplings, with a big tin basin of red, biting chile sauce. But today the school administrators insist on serving Suzanne and me a special lunch. We wait patiently till they call us, imagining a sea of cooks put out by all this extra fuss. Eventually, we're led up to a second-story hallway, dusty with construction. In the middle of its long emptiness stands a table, set with ten dishes for the two of us. No one can be coaxed into helping us with all this food. Everyone vanishes and we sit eating in the sultry afternoon, two women and a banquet floating in the echoes of an empty hallway, a scene Fellini might have dreamed if he could dream in Chinese.

Students: Young men and women in their twenties—but really boys and girls, giggly and romantically naive as freshman in some 1950s high school in the rural Midwest, before the news came through of Elvis and James Dean. One day, a friend from the States mails me a fifties' high school yearbook and my students like the fashions—why not, they look like that too—the same frumpy haircuts and winged glasses, the same white anklets. I ask them to write biographies and get a collection of Chinese self-effacing phrases, threaded through with the sad fear that they'll be assigned to teaching jobs when they dream of being business experts in the world of foreign trade. And then the stiff Party upper lip: "I hope to learn to do the job of teacher well."

No one ever wants to speak in class. Why should they—when their classmates laugh at every English mistake. I let them laugh at my Chinese to prove we're equally inept. I play

35

the clown, bobbing up and down the aisles, demonstrating the Charleston to introduce the 1920s and F. Scott Fitzgerald. I lean over the student who leans head down into her desk, refusing to answer my questions, laughing "I can't, I can't." Good days, I laugh too; bad days, I want to kick her like a cowering dog. The students are used to memorizing teachers' lectures, not to discussing their own thoughts. I give them questions to consider in groups, and when I move around the class, the groups begin to follow me and melt together, till I have one batch of boys and one of girls. One morning, discussing Hemingway, the girls maintain that the macho stoic in "The Snows of Kilimanjaro" is actually weak. I congratulate them on their growing feminism. I put my arm around their giggling heads. In China, an unmarried woman over twenty-eight is considered dead. I'm single and turning forty. For some of my female students I become a sign of hope. Dancing up and down the classroom aisles, I'm too animated to be dead.

One sunny afternoon we hold class outside, and my students are concerned about sitting on the sidewalk, though it's no dustier than their classroom desks. They fuss and barely squat, sitting on the bits of paper that's so scarce in China. Behind us, a man swims in the institute's pool, with its slimy green swamp in the corner, old brooms and mops floating by. We practice Western table manners, preparing for some future dinner with a foreign executive. What would you do with fish bones, I question. Everyone knows you can't spit them on the table or the floor as the people do here, and everyone knows you can't just swallow them, the way the Chinese swallow frustration, known as "eating bitterness," but no one's clear about alternatives to these extremes. Jack Kerouac's extremes seem just as mystifying. One day I teach a chapter from *On the Road*. What does it mean, I ask, to be "on the road"? Imagine that you own an old car. Imagine that you leave your school, your job, your work-unit and assigned apartment. You leave your family. Imagine there are endless superhighways crossing China, and you can drive, not knowing, not caring where. Would you do it? A few adventurous ones are ready. One girl tells me she would sit in the car and think about it for a week.

Eventually, I turn almost as timid and prudish as my students. In a discussion of the English for medical terms, I leave out the ones with sexual connotations. And still I give them a poem by Ntozake Shange with words like "sodomized" and "menses" and "sperm." Inevitably, the questions start: This word's not in my dictionary. What does it mean? By the time we get through defining "sperm," we're all a bit embarrassed but the boys persist. Okay, they say, but why does the poet call it "boiling sperm"? That, I say, is simply what some men like to believe.

Raised Hands: Raised hands in class are rare because no one likes to volunteer an answer. My friend Liana, who teaches in a medical college, turned to face her class the first day, while asking them a question, and thought she was a great success. There were four hands raised at the back of the room. She looked again. The hands were floating in glass cases of formaldehyde.

Payday: A Chinese teacher earns from 60 to 150 yuan a month. I'm paid 850, about 250 dollars U.S. Of course, I also teach more than twice as many hours a week as the Chinese do, but the math still comes up lop-sided, and on paydays everyone tends to forget how many hours I work. On payday, we crowd into the office to pick up our *renminbi*, the local money that gets printed in notes no bigger than a ten. There sits mine, in stacks of a hundred, criss-crossed until the mound is too large for my purse. And before we can leave, the accountants make us stand at the table and count our month's pay.

Sweet Soup: It's Christmas, at least for us foreigners, who take advantage of the holiday no matter what we think about religion. The Chinese also love the chance for a party. Suzanne and I have concocted a tree by stealing bits of branches from the evergreen on the school grounds, decorated it with stars cut from the gold foil that tops our packages of cigarettes. The party's in my office, where even with the cast-iron heater cranked up, everyone is wrapped in padded coats with long underwear slipping out beneath the cuffs and insulated cotton shoes. There's tea, of course, and the foreigners have bought a sort of fruit bread, but the Chinese top us with a cake made entirely of fake cream covered with a cherry jam. Mr. Tang, one of the English department teachers, has brought a steaming sweet soup, thick with mushrooms and peanuts. The words for "sweet" and "soup" are the same in Chinese—*tang* like his name—differentiated only by the tones. So everyone laughs about Mr. Tang's soup, calling it *"Tang de tang tang"* and devouring its sweet warmth. Mr. Tang laughs and chain-smokes, telling his versions of Western jokes, strung together as rapidly as his cigarettes. Everyone must perform. It's a Chinese partytime tradition. The department head is coaxed into a few bars of Chinese opera, professionally delivered with her mouth in a tiny bow. I am beaten into a Western Christmas song: "All I want for Christmas is my two front teeth," faking an appropriately noisy lisp. All the foreigners want for Christmas is to go home. So we do, to the bar at the Jin Jiang Hotel, with its red and green lit tree, its muzak carols on tape.

Style: China's low on fuel. By law, most places south of the Yangtse River go unheated, and the concrete walls house a cold winter damp. My students' ears and fingers swell with purple chilblains. I take off my gloves in class to write with gritty chalk, rub it out with newsprint or a rag. A friend writes that she pictures me in a clinging black jersey sheath, with a cloche hat, smoking in hotel bars. I look down at my December classroom fashions—my sweat pants layered fat with cotton long underwear, my down jacket, my wool beret pulled close over my ears. I wonder what strange misconceptions my letters have conveyed.

Some friends from home send me huge blue padded polar boots, built for relaxing in the tent at a Mt. Everest campsite. My students point and laugh when I wear the boots to class, but I counter with the argument that at least *my* feet are warm, if not fashionable, and anyway, the label states these boots were made in China. But no one has ever seen anything like them in a store. Later, when the spring comes, Peggy and I discover an old woman selling bright flowered and striped cotton pants from a cart in the street. Someone tells us these are really Chinese pajamas, but we don't care. The first day I wear them to school, I come into class early and stand behind the podium. Once the students have taken their seats, I begin my lecture, stepping casually out from behind my cover, pretending for a while not to notice the barely suppressed giggles, knowing the students recognize my stylish pants as proper nightwear.

Minor Changes: To the leaders at my institute, a "minor change" in my schedule means that three of my four classes are suddenly transformed. New material to prepare, another seventy Chinese names to learn. One day, the leaders want to replace my English conversation class with one entitled "The United States." The United States what? I ask, naively. Oh, you know, they reply—history, economics, politics, art, geography, religion—the United States. We have a text, they add. Great, I answer, then you don't need me. Eventually I win the argument, but first I must withstand an onslaught of "persuasive" visits from my new department leader. He places himself like a rock beside my desk, hunched above me in his blue down jacket, making me truly understand the suicides of the Cultural Revolution—understand deep in my blood how a man could drive me into leaping from a fifth-story window and never blink behind his yellow glasses.

Political Action: The classroom lights are centrally controlled. Flip the switch and nothing happens. The school leaders decide when the day is grey enough to turn the current on. My students already wear thick glasses. I already wear contact lenses, what the students call invisible glasses. No one can read the chalkboard; boys in the back of the room borrow a second pair of spectacles, put both pairs on, and still can't see the lesson. I tell the class it's time for action. I write a letter to the leaders, full of phrases about how the progress of the motherland depends upon the 20-20 vision of its future leaders. Most of the students sign the letter, some taking cover by using the English names they give themselves in class. Still, they sign. One class applauds me when I read the letter to them. Everyone enjoys the propaganda about the motherland. A week after I deliver the message, the lights come on at the switch. We're in control. And now I have to teach the students about conservation.

Campaigns: The Chinese government likes campaigns—billboards and posters with the latest slogans, old retired people mustered into the streets with banners and drums. Lately, the campaign has focused on beautification. The school has joined in. The "English for Today" chalkboard is covered with pronouncements about the five beautifications—all Latinate empty generalizations. I'm a writing teacher; I specialize in specifics and the concrete image. So, at the bottom of the board, I add, "Don't spit. Don't blow snot on the street." I wait for the repercussions, but no one mentions the chalkboard to me, though the words stay up there for a week. No one except Paul who rushes into my office, delighted to find that some Chinese student has finally grasped a real command of the situation and of the English idiom.

ENGLISH AS A FOREIGN LANGUAGE

Miss Y is a new young teacher of Chinese. I meet her one day in the school's small, dingy bathroom, her head popping over the half-open stall door, smiling, her round face with the smoothness of steamed dumplings before they're crimped into folds like a drawstring bag. She speaks hardly any English, but descends on me every day now, demanding and bashfully open as a puppy, eager to show her tricks, to read an English passage about pumas. And neither of us has ever seen a puma, but the words are magic, and the ability to pronounce them, to recognize them in this strange flat language that repeats the same regulation signs, unlike her own graceful characters that stretch and swirl upon themselves like carp in a pond. We learn together, trading our foreign sounds. I'm like a child, learning what to call my nose. Each time I look at Miss Y, she pulls her own, asking me in pantomime to name it for myself in Chinese and once again in English for her. Our worlds are what we see and touch: fan, shoes, jeans, purse, the cup and bowl from the school—enamel and ringing when the chopsticks knock the empty bottom—that hollow music making a language of its own, simpler than this other hunger to name, and feed our hearts with words.

CARRIERS OF THE NEWS

Before I came to China, stamp collecting meant the boy who wore a tie to school and Coke-bottle glasses. He grew up to study history and win research grants to find new angles on the Peloponnesian War. My own interest in stamps was negative; when forced to make a choice at the post office, I'd say give me something without the Virgin Mary or a flag. Now, because I've lived a year inside this country, all my life my mailbox will be blessed with letters, the paper delicate as spider webs, the characters across it strange and indecipherable as spider talk, and, best of all, the Chinese stamps.

The Chinese government prints stamps as intricate as scrolls or broad with Soviet-style realism: landscapes, missiles, paper lanterns and cranes, oil derricks in the sunset, a bearded poet beneath the moon. New designs come often, new sets and series. Every shopping street has stores devoted to collectors' needs. Sundays, certain corners of the streets become a market, a place to buy and trade, or just admire.

Nearly every Chinese collects stamps. When my foreign letters arrive, I tear the corners off, horde small stacks to give my friends, my students, and the *fu wu yuan* at my hotel. The foreign stamps turn quickly dull, the same two or three designs. I tell my correspondents to use more imagination at the post office. I tell them stamps are more than gifts; they're also ways to build my *guanxi*, my connections, a little bribe for good will when I need it.

When I give stamps to Mr. Yong, the gift is pure. I ask nothing from this gently humble man, whose politeness makes him shy away as quickly as a fawn. Mr. Yong is one of the messengers the school's leaders use to send the foreign teachers news. The news is mostly bad: more duties outside our contracts, rules recently concocted to squelch our latest requests or plans. The other messenger is Mr. Jin, who bobbles ceaselessly in and out of our offices, asking are we busy, sitting down forever anyway, laughing a stilted ho, ho, ho at his own quips. His constant presence is as evil as the news he brings. A man we don't trust, but the leaders don't trust him either. They use him because he is there to be used, trying to keep his own niche, trying in vain to build one higher up. They use him as a decoy for our anger, hoping we won't look past him into their bushes.

One day the leaders send the messenger too far. Mr. Jin takes some reports from my office, and though I never directly call him a thief, our voices can be heard throughout the school. After that, my only messenger is Mr. Yong. Dr. James, he asks, would you please consider doing this task? No, I say, and tell him why, and promise I'll write a letter to the leaders to explain. I'll say he pleaded with me, but I, like the stubborn foreigner I am, remained unmoved. He smiles, understanding the matter's settled, and then we're free to look at stamps.

My friend Suzanne thinks Mr. Yong was broken in the Cultural Revolution, but these are things we don't discuss with him; we've learned to keep such questions to ourselves. We look at stamps. Many of his were destroyed during the Cultural Revolution, when, unlike now, the government damned hobbies as bourgeois. One man lost his entire collection, worth $30,000. That's a fortune in China, but it's not the loss of money that saddens Mr. Yong. He's a purist, not a capitalist. He loves the stamps, the pleasure and the perfection. He asks us not to cut the edges of the ones we give him—there must be space around the stamp before he soaks it free of the envelope, or it's no good. He graciously brushes away our hands when Suzanne and I reach, ignorant of manners, for his stamps. He gives us a pair of tweezers, explaining that the residue on our skin will harm the stamps. And you smoke, he reminds us. The nicotine on your fingers, you know. Such words are not a scold, but a patient training. I think you like stamps too, he says. And he begins to bring us some of his. Pure gifts.

I think of history professors, picking up bits of ancient wars between their tweezers, magnified through glasses. I think of Mr. Yong, of messengers of gentleness. How, I ask Suzanne, could stamp collecting have been considered dangerous and wrong? She tells me even the tiny houseplants that now grace every Chinese balcony were forbidden in the Cultural Revolution. And grass, she says, the grass was named bourgeois. Destroyed.

SOMEWHERE IN NORTH AMERICA

It's a late January afternoon, cold in the bare concrete school, even in the offices of the *waiguoren*, who in deference to our delicate foreign status are given electric heaters, a bit like cast-iron suitcases, with holes at the top to aim the warmth straight at the ceiling.

An old man enters. We think we've never seen him before but can't be sure. There are so many old men at the school. This one has a letter he wants us to correct. He plans to send it somewhere in North America. It is a letter of application for a job as an English typing teacher. At the school we type on ancient heavy manuals called Flying Fish. They function like a stone with fins. In the letter, the man does not mention Flying Fish. Instead, he writes: "I was a judge of the Shanghai English Typing competition. Perhaps you saw me on television, November 24, 1985, at 5 o'clock?"

My friend Paul corrects the English in the English typing teacher's letter. It is very quiet in the office, and the air around the old man seems fragile, as he waits, patiently, bent a little over Paul's desk. A sliver of late sunlight floats across the wall behind him, yellow as a carp. Swimming west. The long way to North America.

III

Harpo and Karl

MEI YOU

After the dry-heave sound of men hawking up a good spit, the next most constant rhythm in China is *mei you*. Literally translated, it means "not have." In a shop full of Chinese liquors, beer is *mei you*. A bakery lists twelve kinds of mooncakes, the names in red characters on strips of paper fluttering from the ceiling. But I can't read Chinese and the only cake I know the name for is always *mei you*. *Mei you* is my size in shoes, shirts, and pajamas. Only a few years ago, everyone here wore plain grey or navy; now even nail polish is in fashion, and the shops stock plenty of it—red, pink, and sometimes purple—but polish remover remains *mei you*. This kind of *mei you* is a small mystery, linked to the big mystery of Chinese commerce, the supply and non-supply of goods that move by the slow boat of bureaucratic regulations and the small slippery fleet of backdoor trade.

Take beer—*pijiu*. The Shanghai Chinese can't rely on local *pijiu* either—now and then it shows up, purchasable only with a stamped ration coupon. When it comes to the foreigners' tables in a hotel restaurant, the label reads "Imported from Shanghai." Like the Chinese, I learn to settle for a watery sweet orange drink instead, sucking it through a straw, standing beside the shop along with the workers who brewed *pijiu* all day and the ones who stacked the bottles into crates, hauled them to the docks where they wait five weeks because the harbor's backed up and an export ship is *mei you*.

These are small irritations, a kind of shrug-of-the-shoulders *mei you* that everybody shares, like flies in a Midwest August or mosquitoes on a river camping trip. The other kind of *mei you* is harder to take. Enter a restaurant, one minute past seven. The Chinese eat early, so the tables are crowded with people finishing or halfway through their meal. Walk toward the one empty table, and a waitress cuts past, flinging a rude *mei you* like a knife she's just pulled loose from chicken guts. Sit down, and every waitress has the same knife, and it's the only time they move fast, like quick edits in low-budget *kung fu* films, faces averted, hands chopping the air with *mei you*. No one explains. No one cares whether your Chinese language skills could handle an explanation, could understand "We're sorry. The kitchen closed at six or seven or last year and we're just serving the ones who queued up early."

In Shanghai, people spit their fish bones on the table or throw my change across the counter in a scattered wash of crumpled notes, but the same ones can greet me with a sea of bows, formally polite. Language seems less contradictory than action. Before I came here, I told a friend, "The Chinese are so modest, I'll never learn the phrase for 'fuck you.'" Now I understand its rhythms: *mei you, mei you, mei you*. Someone spits. The fish bones stack me up.

THE TEACHER OF *QI GONG*

S unday afternoon, my friend Ming, a young teacher of English, arrives with a teacher of *Qi Gong*—one of those ancient rituals of slow-motion movements, with its roots in a curious mix of healing and the martial arts. Westerners are more familiar with its cousin, *Tai Ji*, with the photographs of Chinese by the hundreds, practicing their pre-dawn *Tai Ji* in a park or square, their gentle answer to aerobics. In *Qi Gong*, one moves even more slowly than in *Tai Ji*. Mostly, Ming tells me, only the sick have the patience for *Qi Gong*. Perhaps it's the effort to achieve that patience that brings them health.

The *Qi Gong* teacher has big ears, the lobes blue from years of winter chilblains, like the ears of so many older Chinese men. He stands at ease, suspended from his cosmic energy, like a puppet on a string, his eyes half closed, the fly on his baggy pants half open. All his bones pop in their sockets as he shifts and swivels in *Qi Gong*, making a strange soft percussion. He set his feet in a wide *plié*, arms and hands drifting up and around, slowly lifting an imaginary bowl to the center that he breathes from, the center where the *qi* sits— that precious energy, that power.

He gives me too many moves at once, never stopping to be sure I've understood. Stops now because I give up for the moment, in wild gestures of frustration. We talk, or rather, Ming translates his stories. He tells us that both the Daoists and the "ordinary people" developed *Qi Gong*, first for health and meditation, later as a fighting tactic. When the *qi*'s called up, he says, your chest turns bullet proof, you can lie on splintered glass, smash a stone against your head and suffer no harm.

Once there was a monk who never slept, only meditated in a *Qi Gong* posture, sitting upright on the edge of his chair, breathing from his diaphragm, his tongue to the roof of his mouth to increase the flow of saliva (good for digestion), his eyes bent down toward his nose, his nose toward his heart. He tied a rope around his head to keep himself from falling over if he happened to doze off.

Now, the legend of how acupuncture began. A forest fire broke out around a village. The falling twigs and pine needles lightly pierced the villagers' bodies, many at the acupressure points. Sick people felt cured. So they began to use sharp stones and, later, needles to duplicate the healing. How, I ask, did they know it was the pine needles and not the fire itself that healed them. Ming declines to translate, considering it another of my humorously impertinent questions she's grown used to by now.

The teacher has also invented a cure—special prescription glasses for nearsightedness. The frames will have knobs placed at the proper acupressure points, and these knobs will be connected to small batteries, providing an electric massage. A marriage of the ancient and high tech.

But he's tired of talking and wants to demonstrate the moves with Ming. They make an unlikely pair, Ming so tall and angular above his tiny compact ease. Now, he's showing the "defense style," asking Ming to push her elbowed weight against his "strong groin," to strike his arm so full of *qi* he feels no pain.

Their faces turn greasy with sweat. The teacher's brought his own towel, and Ming disappears into my bath. Time, the teacher announces, for an acupressure massage. His hands churn on my back, smoother than pine needles, slipping even more smoothly under my bra-less shirt, and suddenly one hand between my breasts, carefully stalking the acupressure canyon, never shifting off its center to the left or right. Still, I wonder is this healing or just a cheap thrill, a chance to cop the sort of foreign feel the local morals won't allow. Times like this I feel unsure outside my culture, wondering whether I should offend or be offended, wondering just how many universals East and West share. Luckily Ming appears from the bath and takes the greasy *Qi Gong* teacher home.

I decide the patience of *Qi Gong* is less than tempting. I decide that I'm not sick enough to learn it.

THE INADVERTENTLY FUNNY

Keys: Six-thirty a.m., the hotel restaurant just opening, Paul at the table, ticking off the minutes till the bus arrives for school. The scrambled eggs come, but the silverware's locked up in the bottom drawer of the heavy wooden cabinet in the corner. And no one has the key. In a country where so little is stolen, keys have nothing to do with crime. They create a kind of surreal sense of order and a freedom from responsibility. It's certain that the chaos is locked up, uncertain who has the key. If, for example, I see something I like in a shop window, inside the clerks will say the item's sold out. No matter, I say, I'll buy the one in the window. But the window is behind a door. Locked up. And the owner of the key is ill or out to lunch, or perhaps, conveniently, the key's been lost, and once they locked the window, they've never had to change displays. Goods like shoes and sweaters are not vital. They can live forever in the window, and the clerk is happy not to have to fetch them, not to interrupt a good session of gossip to ring up a sale. But the Chinese hold a reverence for food. Something must be done about the eggs on Paul's table. Somehow the waiters find an axe, more readily available than keys. They hack the cabinet till the bottom splinters and the forks cascade onto the floor. They pick one up, triumphant. They bring it to Paul's table.

Lamp Chains: Next to my bed stands a small chest with a built-in console of buttons designed to summon service people, music, and the lights. Most of its connections are dead, but it does trigger the bedside light, operating in tandem with the lamp's chain. One day, the chain stops working. My maid calls hotel maintenance, and two men arrive, carrying a new lamp. It seems a reasonable solution—to replace the wrecked one with a functional twin. I'm wrong again. Painstakingly, the men dismember my lamp and the new one—and switch the chains.

Public Relations: One day my hotel installs a desk in the main lobby, names it Public Relations. Sometimes a person sits there, behind the potted plant and the brochures that advertise a hotel club and swimming pool that workers bulldozed to nothing a year ago. The third January week that I've gone without heat, I find a man behind the desk, friendly, in a suit. While we wait for some report from maintenance, he asks me how I find the service here. Normally I'd lie and say it's fine and everyone would save face. But this is not a good afternoon and so I tell the truth. "It's terrible," I say, "the worst hotel in China." "Really," he replies, seemingly amazed. "And how long have you lived in this hotel?" "Six months," I say. "Six months," he echoes. "And you have already formed your opinion?"

Eggs Again: Paul's Chinese vocabulary is minimal, but his patience is abundant. One morning he orders what is known as a Western breakfast—white toast and two fried eggs. The waitress returns with two plates, four eggs, sunny-side. The next morning, Richard, another teacher, joins Paul at the breakfast table and orders the Western eggs. Paul warns him, but Richard waves the problem off, pointing out how well he, unlike Paul, can speak Chinese. The waitress leaves and Richard settles into satisfaction, another Chinese hurdle leaped.

His back is to the kitchen. Only Paul can see the waitress coming now with Richard's breakfast, five plates balanced in her arms— a Western month of eggs.

Long Underwear: In winter, China's need to husband its energy resources means there's no heat allowed south of the Yangtse River, other than the random warmth that sometimes graces foreigners' rooms. In the damp concrete homes of a country that must build without trees, long underwear is a must. It comes in cotton colors on the local shelves, in silk for the foreign shops. Silk seconds sometimes appear in the local stores; the word goes out and the stock is sold within an hour. All winter the cuffs of it peek out below the hand-knit sweaters, jeans, and shapeless jackets. And all spring. And mid-May, well into Shanghai's humid heat, I see those winter cuffs below the pants of sweating men, busy on construction sites. There must be an official day to shed that inner skin. The weather doesn't count, only the rules of custom. Today, I'm sunning in my swimsuit, scandalous on the hotel lawn, with Chinese couples around me in sweaters, posing for a photo beside this tree, that bit of grass. Mr. Hao, a young writer, comes to visit wearing a navy blue suit, a sweater vest, a long-sleeved shirt, and tie. I make him sit on the grass, but I give up the sun, put on a modest shirt. Slowly, he sheds his coat, at last the sweater too. There are rules and weather. We make these compromises.

An English Lesson: Some Shanghai boys cry "hel-lo" in a teasing sing-song every time I pass them on the street. It's their equivalent of construction workers' tongue clicks back home in the States, their wolf-whistles and "hey babe." And it's the only English word they know. So one day I answer "fuck off," and the words come back in sing-song, a mimic innocent as a parrot's. I laugh, thinking of all the English-speaking foreigners who'll walk here, the buses of elderly tourists, their genteel ears rolling by, listening for those sweet and humble Oriental tones, that tourist China they've paid so much to visit, under glass.

Tablecloths: Ming takes me to dinner, a state restaurant with the typical short dining hours: five p.m. to seven. The place is just opening, but they let us in anyway. The waiters sit, reading newspapers, cleaning their fingernails at the tables. Sometime after five, they begin to set the tables up, covering the large ones with white cloths. Ming asks for a cloth. There are only two of you, the waiter says, why should you want a tablecloth? But our table's dirty, so we pressure him and we get a smudged bedsheet, folded up and laid across the wood. We're pleased enough, and ready to order food. In these restaurants, a diner pays before the meal comes. Despite the paper shortage in China, where few forests grow, our waiter writes three separate bills, with three copies of each. One for food, with a charge for the room's air conditioning factored in like tax, one for our drinks. And the third we can't decipher. Ming asks the waiter. It's the fee for the tablecloth.

Weddings: Peggy's brought only one formal dress to China, and it's decadently backless. Today she has to wear it to a Chinese wedding and takes three buses across town to borrow my shawl. We knot it carefully around her shoulders, draped well below her waist in back, but there is nothing we can do about her long blonde hair. The crowds still gather; the bride is still upstaged.

The Better Part of Valor: The Seaman's Club has Guinness on tap sometimes, and sometimes Janis Joplin tapes. Tonight Peggy and I are the only women in a wash of sailors—Greeks and Indonesians from the same ship. They dance with each other, Zorba style and disco, but suddenly the dance turns sour and a fight starts. Peggy and I pay no attention, accustomed to a world of Western bars, where third-string running backs moonlight as bouncers. When a chair breaks and a glass flies past our heads, we understand how easily assumptions can be wrong. The only biceps rippling here are salty. Two Chinese waiters have crouched down behind the bar; the rest are gathered outside the door, risking an occasional glance to check the action. The room erupts in chairs and bottles. We choose the Chinese as our people, make a line drive for the door.

Making Plans: Paul knows a Chinese man who plans. He buys a load of watermelons because the season's right and every corner holds a crowd of people eating, tossing rinds into straw baskets. But then the temperature drops, not far enough to be cold, but far enough for the Chinese to decide that fruit so pink and watery would be unwholesome. The load of melons rots. The man remains undaunted. He has a bigger plan, is eager to emigrate to the States, the country of big planners. He has heard that dental care there is expensive. He takes precautions. He has all his teeth pulled.

Telephone Backtalk

Ni hao makes a greeting, a friendly "hi, how are you" to a neighbor met on the street, a student passing in the hall. *Wei* functions in a more utilitarian manner. Coming in a quick succession—*wei, wei, wei*—it works as a warning, an attention grabber: "look out, I'm about to run you over" or "stop, come back, don't do that." One nasally delivered *wei* is how the Chinese answer phones, a sort of acknowledgment, an announcement that they're on the line. Sometimes a multitude of *wei*s bounce back and forth until one party gives up and says something else; sometimes the Chinese keep responding *wei* no matter what I tell them.

Chinese long distance often disconnects at random, or the voice disappears mid-sentence, then returns. One night Peggy calls from Beijing to tell me which hotel to meet her in. I can hear her and the Beijing operator but no one can hear me; no one knows I'm shouting *wei* into the line. They give up, call again. Same problem. Third try, the line carries all our voices, and the Shanghai operator too. Quick, Peggy, say your hotel's name, before some crow lands on the miles of wire between us, short-circuiting our plans.

I punch the button on my hotel phone to get an outside line. Maybe I hear seven voices talking *wei*, maybe alternating beeps. Maybe I hear the right tone, so I dial and nothing happens. I hang up. The phone rings, jangling at me. I answer, nobody there. Only myself calling myself—the futile echo of the number dialed out, boomeranging home.

THE TWELVE-*KUAI* DWARF

Hangzhou is what we all thought China would be like. A big lake lies at the city's edge, circled by tree-lined walks and formal gardens with graceful carved pavilions. Two causeways slice the lake, built by emperors and poets centuries ago. Here and there the causeways rise into small curved bridges with fantastic beasts carved in stone. Men sit fishing under the willows, the tips of their bamboo poles propped on forked sticks planted in the water. Islands pattern the lake, with small ponds built to reflect the moon; long, low wooden boats pole past. Hills rise on three sides, and the pagodas make tall shadows in the constant mist.

I take a bus to Long Jin—the Dragon Well—where people stir the water in a murky pool to watch the flecks of silver rise and call them dragon money. Women along the road hawk the famous Long Jin tea, looking for another kind of silver.

Behind the well, a path climbs steeply into the hills, terraced with tea bushes. Boulders and stone outcroppings cluster on the facing hills like a random, animated cemetery. What looks like river veins tracing the slopes are stone steps, each slab carried up on shoulder poles. The valley stretches green and brown below and I stop to rest among the scrub pines, each needle pearled with mist. I feel a little vertigo, feel strangely frightened. For months I haven't walked in my own Northwest mountains, only in the densely human streets of Shanghai, and like a good Chinese, I feel uncertain without a crowd, with all this unfamiliar quiet broken only by some tiny, white-jowled birds, cracking pine seeds in a two-part rhythm.

And yet I'm not Chinese enough. I still resent the sudden old man on the path beyond me, cutting brush beside the tea rows, bundling it in two enormous loads. Just before I fade back into the fog, he looks up, starts to talk. I don't speak Chinese well, and this is Hangzhou dialect, different from the Mandarin tones in my *Elementary Chinese Reader*. I hate repeating *ting bu dong* (literally, "hear but don't understand"), and hate repeating yes without a sense of what I might be promising.

The old man is short and wiry. Torn socks, torn pants, the red-brown soil rubbed into his clothes and his gloves with the fingers cut out. Under his cap his hair seems dusted with steel filings, like an actor made up for a part, not as if the hair has truly grown grey. His round, flattened face is open, friendly behind the usual crooked, yellow teeth.

His arm swings out to name the tea rows. I think he's telling me to buy some tea, and when I'm home I'll dream of Long Jin farms. But his limbs are thin as each stick in the bundles he's lifting on his shoulders and I don't want to dream of this humiliation, remember how I didn't want to turn back yet, didn't want to drag a bundle down the hill, and still I had to offer. And remember his refusal. I have to dog behind him anyway, politely, while he struggles with his load and keeps refusing help. And now I think he's asked me home to taste the good tea. So I say yes and have to run to keep up with his sudden bobbing step, a fast downhill march, counter-pointed with grunts.

I think he must be pleased to bring this foreign woman home. I like his hospitality, the way he leads me through the back paths of the village, past the neighbors coming out to comment. At his home, I meet his wife, what must be a married daughter, and a grandson. This I expect, but not the dwarf, round as a child in his layered smock, watching me from behind the sad banana he slowly peels and mouths as slowly, the fruit half-forgotten, all his taste buds in his eyes now.

I'm seated in their kitchen, on a low bamboo chair, under a hanging basket of plucked chicken. The old man bustles in and out, changing his clothes. His ungloved hands are steel grey as his hair.

The wife takes over. The wife has steel in her spectacled glance and her will. She measures green tea in a glass, pours boiling water. Before it brews, she starts her hard sell. Two kinds of tea leaves in her shallow basket—these costlier leaves are better. To me, her words seem mostly *ting bu dong*, but like the dwarf, I understand the pantomime. I hate green tea. I know I have to buy some to assuage my guilt, to stop the nightmare of that old man weighted down with dragging bush and me behind him, empty handed. Half a *jin* costs twelve *kuai*; I agree to buy that. The old man's disappeared again, and the woman's shoving tea inside a too-small box. I'd tell her never mind the extra leaves, but she's not pleased that I won't buy more and I have to pretend to want my money's worth. Without that pretense, I'm naked as the plucked chicken draped above my head or the banana in the dwarf's fat hand beside me.

I'm so foreign I know nothing, but I understand when visits become foreign trade. The tea steeping in my glass is forgotten. The wife lights a candle, seals the plastic bag around my purchase, running the wick along a file at the bag's top. It's time to pay.

A foreigner should carry the crisp, desirable foreign exchange, but I work for China and get paid in local *renminbi*. When I pull it out, the wife is angry, and the old man, with some greater sense of forgiveness, looks simply sad. He escorts me to the bus stop, where I board and ride off into misty distance, dwindling in his vision, like a twelve-*kuai* dwarf.

LEARNING THE SYSTEMS

B ureaucracy: System number one. An ancient Chinese
habit. Perhaps now part of the country's gene pool.
Infinitesimal degrees of petty power, fiercely clung to.
Committees inside committees, repeating like the girl on the
Morton Salt box, and time-worn as that image. Rules impossible to count as all the grains inside the box, and new ones
concocted on the spot to stop whatever enterprise you've suddenly dreamed up. A tangible presence and yet no word for
it inside my pocket Chinese dictionary. No way to frame the
question: who's in charge?

Back-biting: A child of number one, or perhaps its parent. In
the third century BC, the poet-statesman Qu Yuan was dis-
missed from the emperor's court because he complained about
back-biting political intrigue. Disappointed that he could not
save the country from corruption, he drowned himself in
Hunan's Mi Luo River. However the people feel about their
statesmen, they love their poets. They filled bits of hollow
bamboo with rice, and took a boat to search for Qu's body,
throwing the rice into the river to lure the fish away, to keep
them from devouring Qu Yuan. Now that ritual food is eaten
on the fifth day of the fifth lunar month—glutinous rice with
red bean paste or meat, wrapped in bamboo leaves, neat tri-

angles tied with reeds. Stomachs profit from disasters of cruel mouths. But last week when a teacher jealously informed on a co-worker for moonlighting as an interpreter, the moonlighter had to give up the money she'd earned. And no one threw rice.

Guanxi: The sweeter side of intrigues, *guanxi* translates easily as "pull"—connections, favors one can call in—gained by good-will, power, or ingratiation. Because all the Chinese love to collect stamps, I earn *guanxi* by saving the canceled corners of my foreign letters. I increase it when I loan my favorite hotel maid my shawl, to let her knit a copy. Xiao Wang has inherited *guanxi*; she can get us tickets to a play because her father is a literary *ganbu*, which translates as important person.

Hai Kou Men: Means "open the back door," the wise way to deal with any bureaucratic system. If you have the money for the luxury of your own telephone, it can still take six months, maybe longer, to get your line hooked up. Use the back door, start receiving calls tomorrow. Rarely so crass as bribes, the back door's mostly *guanxi*—a friend, a connection somewhere in whatever system you need. In a country strung together by one official language but where most people speak a homelier dialect, the back door is the mother tongue, and bureaucracy is a second grammar people learn only in order to circumvent its rules. One rule says whatever high tech comes in with a foreigner must also leave. But my bags are overloaded for the plane already and I don't want to take my bulky Smith-Corona home. The back door brings me a buyer. We walk together out of my hotel, me toting the case so the guards at the gate won't think my friend's a buyer, or a thief. Then I circle back through a different gate, so the guards won't see me empty-handed. Like the Chinese opera, everything moves by disguise and plots.

Communism: My second disillusionment—after learning that

the scene at the Peace Hotel was not like *Casablanca*, that the band played forties' jazz like stumbling drunks (only worse because they played it sober) and the foreign community held no Bogart. The country isn't classless. Hierarchies remain, as old as the days of the long-fingernailed Mandarins: four classes of tickets on a train, maybe eight on a boat, a ranking over who eats in which school dining hall, a different charge for the same food paid in people's money or foreign exchange. Every man smokes, but not the special brand of cigarettes made only for the Central Party Committee or the even more special brand produced for only Deng Xiao Ping. My Marxism's pure as the page it's never been successfully lifted from, a Dylan and Lennon sixties' vision of a country where the people cheerfully sweep the streets because they own them. Here the worker in the state market would never bring the price of tomatoes down, because he'd have to ask someone's permission to do it and then he'd have to unload the truck, and he'd rather let the fruit rot. In my definition, communism means each person's responsible for the country, but here the "individual responsibility system" is the new and vaguely capitalist economics being tested. Still, I hear some responsible young men dreamed up this economic experiment, sincerely hoping it would help the motherland. Coming from the States, I think it means that people won't work, except for selfish profits. I know it means the only freedom here's the freedom now to buy things. A foreign capitalist who's traded a long time with China tells me business is easier now—better communication systems, better travel—but some of the old Marxist care and quality control have been lost; nobody takes the extra measure to ensure them.

The country's troubles have nothing to do with communism, a mere overlay on the centuries of what's Chinese, where the oldest red is red tape, bureaucracy, and Mandarin fingernails, the safety of making your niche and staying there, of saying yes and yes, and, if you're lucky, finding a back door to do what you please instead.

The Museum of the Chinese Revolution sums it up. First, come the photos of the terrible suffering under feudal and foreign rule—a man bent under a weight of coal; the bodies of starved children. Then the Long March, the ragged string slippers left by those not already barefoot, the pictures of Lu Xun and other revolutionary artists. So many military mementos, I remember the war went on a long time. Then the banners, the posters of Mao hauling the country out of hunger and domination, earning his emperor-like worship. And at the end of the display, a sign saying "no admittance," another sign barring the use of a door. This is what those real and solid liberations have come to, the old barriers, walk this way, think this direction. Follow the long pointed fingernail.

Patience: A virtue I've never liked and like it even less here. When my Chinese friends advise me to have patience, they don't mean wait and the thing you want will come. They mean give up, "eat bitterness"—a system I never learn.

Trust: What there was of it is worn thin now by years of Cultural Revolution. But the home-grown lack of it makes foreigners repositories of trust. I gather secrets every day—the place a friend will travel on her holiday, the dreams of studying in the States, the little secret that the two of us are having dinner together tonight, outside the eyes of watchful colleagues and neighbors. Outside the world of work and politics, the trust goes on. It's the woman in the old city of Dali, side-saddle on the back of a bike, trusting her husband's skill over the ruts, trusting so much she doesn't even hold on to his waist, only to the chicken in the basket on her lap.

Manners: Alternately polite and rude, obsequious and superior. We all use and lose them. Ed and Linda, two teachers from Seattle, give a banquet lunch for a Chinese couple and the family. But it's not expensive enough and the wife asks pointedly if she can eat the kids' leftovers. By definition, everyone's polite to foreigners, and by definition, every foreigner is rich, and so it's open season on their wallets, slim or fat. And somewhere beyond manners is the shop clerk who knows my language skills can't handle her directions and walks me down the block to the store I need and orders for me.

Saving Face: The point of manners and what we try when we've lost them. The oldest habit. The heart of all the other systems.

THE *KE YI* WOMEN

K*e yi* makes a useful phrase. Depending on how it's said, it means "okay? may I?" or "okay, you may." To Peggy and me, *ke yi* means a visit to our Shanghai tailor.

A visit takes nearly a day. In the morning I walk about a mile from my hotel, wearing sunglasses even on rainy days to fight construction dust. I jam onto a bus, ride an hour across Shanghai to Hong Kou Park. Another bus and a walk to Peggy's school. We eat lunch. The next bus takes us near the tailor. We have to count the stops each time because the streets here look so identical, sometimes even to the Chinese. Now we walk past concrete homes with one or maybe two rooms, turn down the alley where the tailor's shop sits just behind the sign for the public phone stall.

Sometimes we find our tailor frying a fish, with bits of shallot. Some days she comes bustling in from an errand down the street or sits gossiping with a neighbor while she whips a seam beneath her old machine's quick needle. Small and bony as a friendly witch, she laughs when she sees us, laughs harder when she sees the clothes we've brought for her to copy: the big full Dolman sleeves, the plunging necklines, the almost backless dresses. Like my friend Xue who sewed me a blouse so modest I couldn't fit my head or arms through the holes, our tailor has her own opinions about style—and tries to impose them. We shake our heads and point again to the clothes laid out across the fabric. Did we buy enough meters? Can you copy this? Everything takes place in pantomime because Peggy and I speak only Mandarin and our tailor only Shanghai dialect. But we share the phrase *ke yi*. The tailor draws a quick pattern with her finger along the cloth. *Ke yi*? We nod, *ke yi*. Exchanges like this form a visit. So we're never quite sure what she'll make. Once I brought a pair of wide-legged pants that needed to be taken in around the waist. I got a pair of riding jodhpurs.

The shop's a dusty jumble of clothes and fabrics, bags of work to be completed and work done. The door always stands open to the street, and the neighborhood drifts in. No dressing rooms. No fittings. One day, the tailor won't believe me when I show her where I've pinned the waistline on a skirt. Perhaps she thinks no foreigner could be that thin. I'm ready to undress to show her I can fit inside the waist, when the man who lives next door wanders in. Our vocabulary fails us. *Ke yi* won't handle this situation. Finally, the man understands our gestures and the laughing tailor. He exits, laughing too. I undress, slip on the skirt. *Ke yi*? Our tailor is convinced. *Ke yi*.

The world of Chinese tailoring is whimsical, made more so by the shortage of good buttons, the lack of zippers in any shade but white. A week before I leave for the States, I find a shop with zippers in pastels, rich browns, and navy. Just before I buy the whole collection, I remember I'm going home. Sometimes we find our tailor's whimsy—or necessity—annoying. Sometimes, a sweet surprise: the pockets of my black trousers are lined with silk pink roses.

We like our tailor. And we think she likes us. In the late afternoon, we walk down the alley, ready for the many bus rides home. We hear her laughing with the neighbors, her black uncombed hair bobbing above her own shapeless uniform blue cotton jacket. We call ourselves the *ke yi* women. We hope she calls us okay too.

BREAD

T he sweet white taste, a soft dough sticking to my teeth and gums, the roof of my mouth. I see the same pale yeastiness in the men's thighs beneath their summer shorts, thin but more pasty than lean. Brown bread exists primarily as rumor, a bit of lore passed on by long-time foreigners to new ones, hungry for the texture of wheat. For a month, one bakery makes the slim dark loaves. Once a week, maybe twice, a few appear on the shelf just before the bakery closes for the evening. One day the shop is gone, the block where it stood now a tangle of wires and crumbling half-walls. China reconstructs.

My street is famous for its bakeries, three within one block. Easy to visit every day. Easy still to come home hungry, every bin beneath glass counters empty, empty racks behind the gossiping clerks. The crowds still fight their way in, old women waiting like me before the bins, staring as if our eyes could fill them. People stand in the corners eating cream cakes, drinking glasses of coffee beige with milk. When bread does arrive, I buy too much, delighted, and in a kind of panic. I eat a loaf on the way home, wrap the rest in plastic to ward off cockroaches, knowing I'll eat the loaves too fast, worrying they'll turn stale, feeling the yeast rising in my own thighs.

71

A Chinese line is usually shapeless, milling forward from the center and the edges. The line outside the Jing'An Bakery is more orderly and always long. Inside, the same elbowing chaos that fills any shop. A joint-venture, fueled by foreign money and tastes, the Jing'An bakes croissants and French loaves. The bakery has one door for people paying local money and one for customers with foreign exchange. The second door never has a line. I load my orange backpack: croissants for me, for Carl and Kelly, my New York friends who bake pizza in return, French loaves for Ming, whose tastes are foreign but not her money.

Once, in Tianjin, Ed and I biked through street markets, the air so full of winter coal-stove soot, we wiped our faces and the cloth turned black. We found good round wheels of bread at a curb stall, bought so many the handles on our plastic bag tore, and a loaf dropped.

Chinese children wear split pants; their parents hold them up, legs spread, to pee on the street. Our bread was soaking in a damp stain. The whole market was watching the two foreigners, the small puddle under the bread not visible from where the watchers stood.

China sponsors propaganda campaigns against litter, with banners and posters, old retired women and men half-heartedly beating drums. Ed and I believe in those campaigns, trust them more surely than our Chinese friends who smile and spit their watermelon seeds across the floor. We have to pick the bread up gingerly, walk—with all the grace of Harpo Marx and Chico—to the tiny garbage box, and toss that good round bread away, in front of the incredulous crowd.

Dragon Che, The Monkey Queen

Before I left the States, I'd always planned to buy a bike, looking at my Chinese calendar on the wall, the photo for January with a crowd of fat-tired green one-speeds lined up in a corner parking lot, something finer than cars at a shopping mall. I'd be Chinese and travel like them.

Then I arrived in Shanghai, and a bike seemed suicide: the random heavy traffic, fleets of bikes and buses, cabs darting between, pedestrians crossing against them all. Only the autumn weather's convinced me, sunny afternoons I know won't last, and I'll be sorry that I spent them in my room or jammed inside a bus.

No shopping here's done quickly. I make some false starts, find one model that seems possible, but not quite what I'd imagined. I'll come back in the morning I say and probably buy it. Loyal to the end, I do, and find it's sold to some other foreign woman at my hotel. Maybe a breakdown in the language; maybe we all look alike. I try another shop, another used bike, but the tiny, aged salesman tells me it has problems, and he'll fix it first. Tells me come back *mingtian*, tomorrow. And I do. And I do again. And I wait a few more days, and it's still *mingtian*. Finally, I try another bike, walk it through the crowded sidewalk, through the street torn up for reconstruction, the muddy puddles and jagged concrete and hoses, and swing up over its male bar, onto the too-high seat at People's Square. It's China and I'm cycling—past the volleyball games, the young man teaching his girlfriend to ride, running along beside her, holding the fender.

Sunset's coming on, and no Chinese bike has lights. Quickly, I decide this one will do, though it's too tall and the wrong gender. But when I enter the shop, a young couple enters beside me with a bike they want to sell—a small one, with no masculine bar. Suddenly, I'm filling out the papers, like registering the title on a car. The couple's smiling, and the old salesman, and me in the center, as if some journalist had posed us. I've bought a bike.

And somehow riding home on busy Yanan Lu seems easy, even in the dark. I'm ringing the bell, cutting in and out between the walkers, like any native cyclist, the fat tires stable at a stop, even before my toes reach down for ground.

I always name machines my life relies on. Back home, I've named my Volkswagen, my printer and computer. Now I name my bike. I call her Dragon Che, The Monkey Queen, because the Monkey King's my favorite character in Chinese opera, because dragons seem synonymous with China, and Che is for Guevara, the sort of guerrilla bike I'll need to brave the streets. The androgyny of this composite feels right.

I kneel in the walkway in front of my hotel, trying, with a nail file and tweezers, to attach the lock that fits around the tire. It opens with a key that rides securely in the lock and slips out easily when I park. A fine Chinese invention, and one that only holds the back tire, doesn't chain the bike to anything. A perfect mark for thieves back home. But not inside this honest country, where my Chinese friends say any person carrying a locked bike home would be suspected.

Tomorrow's a shining autumn Sunday. I'm Chinese at last, riding the details of the city that I've never glimpsed from buses, my orange pack slung across my shoulders, riding back in the darkening streets, under the new bridge, with the sparks from construction torches showering around me like fireworks.

By Thursday, leaving a party with my British friend Steve at two a.m., Dragon Che has a flat. We walk her home through the shadowy quiet of streets I swear I'll ride again for this early morning emptiness, and never do.

But what to do about the flat? I ask some guys at the taxi service, and they decide to fix it, ten of them standing around, one getting dirty. He removes the tire, and then the inner tube, kneading it through a bowl of water to find the leak, sealing it with a scrap of rubber. They won't take payment, and when I ride back with a bottle of wine, they won't take that, until I set it down, lying that I never drink such stuff, and leave.

Che's tires become a ritual. Each time I ride, I have to get them pumped up. I learn that bike mechanics set up shop along the streets, like market vendors, like tailors and the old women who sell eggs boiled in tea. I know them by the tires slung around a street lamp or a tree.

Still, I love every rusting inch of Dragon Che, rusting further in the winter damp outside my door. The sound of bike bells becomes China.

THE CARP'S GENES

For the last two weeks, buses have come less often, their schedules erratic. Chang, one of the teachers, tells me the drivers are unhappy with the rationale behind the latest selective doling out of raises. So the drivers have staged a "sort of" strike, missing work, idling on the job. "We Chinese are like that. We'll get our anger out and the strike will be done." Unions here, but every union works for the government, no real bargaining tables.

Riding the slow bus to a bonsai exhibition, I think this is a bonsaied form of strike. Even the landscape has that quality, composing itself in spare ways, a few jagged rocks, an accent of bent branch. An artist sees a crane inside a tree root, shapes the root enough to let the crane suggest itself, but not fly. Sometimes, people pick their public words as carefully as roots. Or drivers expend their anger in erratic schedules, the suggestion of a strike. The country's stylized like its art, aesthetics shading over into the pragmatism of existing with bureaucracy and few resources. The perfected stroke of the brush across a silk scroll matches the way a Chinese clerk can take a scrap of paper and fold it around some item into a neat package, without the aid of tape or string. Such methods also shape the chaos till it hardly seems chaotic or at least resolves itself around this shaping, the way a straw market basket becomes visual rhythms of the things bought—the tail of a thin silver fish, three eggs, the green wisps of shallots.

In the market, crowds of tiny Chinese carp tred water in flowered basins; big orange ones swim in formal gardens, sucking the tops of ponds. I read they have a gene that makes them sensitive to what they live in, governs how large they grow by the container's size.

CURES

I'm always sick in China. Not from the food. I gain weight, envy my foreign male friends who eat and every day turn thinner. It's my throat that's bad and my lungs. Bronchitis becomes a way of life. The cold, the concrete damp, the smoggy air, my cigarettes. I'm familiar at the school clinic, asking every week for packets of vitamin C. I'm familiar at the hospital, where I park my bike, walk the dingy, ill-swept corridor past the clinic where Chang tells me the "ordinary people" are served, to the waiting room for foreigners and *ganbus*—the upper class of the Chinese. The doctors, in love with 1950s technology, want to put my chest endlessly inside an x-ray. The nurses, in smudged white, smile and stab my finger. Every blunt recycled needle could be hepatitis.

When the doctor wants to run more tests, I pretend to know less Chinese than I do, and she surrenders, paging through her English crib, unable to find the words. We agree on penicillin. We agree on bottles of sweet syrup and Chinese pills, taken always in large doses—eight at once, ten times a day. The nurse packs them in a precious plastic bag with the hospital's name across it. I practice the words to get the name right, imagining the day the crowded bus will win, my crushed ribs will puncture my lung, and I'll whisper "Hua Dong Yi Yuan" before I faint.

My Chinese friends name different cures: Drink egg yolks in a glass with water. Don't eat fresh pears—they bring a chill. One day my constant cold is worse and Chang is worried. She brings me medicine selected by her mother, a doctor of traditional Chinese cures. Inside Chang's neatly wrapped green packet is a mix that looks as if she's traveled to a forest, scooped up the dark, slightly damp and crumbly earth—half composed of seed hulls, pine needles, bark, and spongy fungus—a material somewhere between its original self and decay into loam. I think it's a good witch's brew, healthy and a little scary. I add water and it seethes in the pot, the bubbles not breaking through to the surface. Instead, the thick dark mass heaves up and down, slowly breathing. Full boil is a small eruption, alive, organic. I pour the root brown liquid from the loam. Four bitter swallows. Every day in China, this need to get beyond the taste of fear, this constant lifting to the lips in trust.

IV

Between Language and
Actual Time

TRAIN SKETCHES

Tickets: No return fares sold in China. When I arrive somewhere, my first assignment is to fight the lines to buy a ticket out. Four ticket classes: hard seat, soft seat, sleepers also soft and hard. The descriptions are precise. But my Chinese language skills are not. In Louyang, I forget the word for sleeper, remember I've seen Suzanne say "hard," then fold her hands and lay her cheek against them. I try it, and the woman selling tickets imitates my pantomime, a gentle tease.

A ticket remains essential, even after it's been punched to let you past the boarding gate. On the train, attendants will want to check it again, take it from you if you're in a sleeper, return it just before your stop. Don't drop it, even then. To get out the gate at your destination, you must show the ticket to the person at the turnstile. This is known as giving people jobs.

Waiting: Display the right sort of ticket and you can enter the separate room for those who ride soft. Sometimes just a foreign face will do. The big crowded rooms for hard seat passengers hold all the dirt and desperateness of travel—bodies sleeping on the benches, boxes of candy and mooncakes beside them, clothes tied up in bundles or bulging from the plastic red, blue, and white striped Chinese luggage. Good weather days, hard seat riders wait outside in shifting lines that sit or stand, the station yard like an encampment. I tried to get in line once, but the train attendant wouldn't let me, even though I waved my hard seat ticket. He walked me straight across the square and rang the bell ten minutes at the soft seat door until it opened. To let a foreigner stand among those padded green coats and the shapeless bundles would mean a loss of face for China.

Boarding: First, a mystery, then a panic. What platform will the train leave from? Will it be announced? Will I catch the words for Shanghai, Beijing, the difference between "delayed" and "now"? The trains don't sit long in the station, leave on time, exact as Mussolini's. When one arrives, some hard seat Chinese passengers toss bags to hands draped out the windows, grab the same hand to climb up the steel sides and squeeze in. Passengers who use the doors may find they have to stand up for the whole ride.

Soft Seat: Stuffed, cloth-covered seats, arranged in facing groups of four. Crocheted doilies on the table and draped over the seat's back. Tea cups with lids to hold the heat. Sometimes a potted plant. On a trip to Hangzhou, a Chinese man tells me he escaped to Hong Kong years ago, because he hates communism. I don't, and though we speak in English, this is not a conversation I'd like overheard. When we arrive, I watch him fold his hands, bowing to me humbly, formally goodby. And the communists beyond him, casual, standing straight.

Coming back from Zhenjiang, four foreigners playing cards, Jenny from New Zealand improvising the rules. And then the sudden brakes, tea cups flying across the car. The train moves on ten minutes later. Xiao Wang, an assistant assigned to our travel group, comes back to our compartment to say we hit a young man crossing in the dark countryside. We argue that it can't be true, the train moved on too quickly, didn't stop long enough to call police, an ambulance. Xiao

Wang's small pretty face shows all the horror of messages she seems too young to have to carry—"They say it happens often, and the train can't wait or another train will ram it. The man was dead. Someone from the train got off to take charge." All the way back to Shanghai, Martin's face stays white and silent, visible sum of what we feel.

Hard Seat: Xi'an to Louyang. Mountains, knife-edged plateaus, canyons and jagged peaks—every possible inch farmed. Cave homes in the clay-hard soil, their carved doors arched sometimes like gothic churches, the red paper strips of characters and pictures for the New Year pasted around the entries. Here and there, a chimney rises from a cave. The same landscape Mao's army weathered in, waiting. Once I see a cave home in a cliff face, beside it a ragged dark tree with pale lilac blooms, and a white horse. I expect Zapata to walk out and mount. Graves scatter the fields or lie vulnerable and quiet beside the tracks, some of their mounds piled with rocks. On top, a few sticks are strung with white paper streamers or bedraggled wreaths.

In eight and a half hours, we cover seventy-five miles. No one will suspect I took these photos from a train. Not a hint of a blur.

Midnight. Suzanne and I board hard seat out of Guilin to Kunming. The train's already traveled a day south from Shanghai, thirty-six hours to go. Every seat's filled and the aisles. People sprawl, sleeping in the wet and filth of hours, the kind of desperate scene that must describe evacuations from a war zone. My throat's alive with fever. I resign myself to standing up a day and a half, placing my mind some distance far outside my body. But two soft sleepers are open. We don't care what they cost. We buy them.

Soft Sleeper: In the top bunk, strung with harness to hold me in, I rock along the rails, think of Whitman—"out of the cradle, endlessly...." Later, I wake again, lie with my face to the window, imagining I see snow, but it's just a trick of the lights on passing stone. And are these stars or just a dome of sparkling reflections? In the bunk across from me, a Hong Kong woman watches too. Our eyes meet; we say nothing. Music blasts early from the train's loudspeakers; the attendants knock, shoving open our door. We dress in the dark with a moon and the sun rising. Breakfast in the dining car, a bowl of noodles with tiny shrimp floating on top. Out the window, brown hills, valley fields, and rugged stone. I'm happy, remembering my train rides as a girl in Illinois—the Panama Limited, City of New Orleans to Chicago, breakfasts on white linen with silver teapots and the waiter's gold-toothed smile. Relative to that, soft sleeper's hell; relative to hard seat, name it heaven—despite the guy who spits all day, deep dredging his chest, the squat trough toilet turning steadily to piss and stench, the floor mop stuffed in the sink.

Control: The train attendants have it: the power to the fan in soft seat on a summer ride, the switch that starts the sudden Beijing opera on the speakers in the pre-dawn. The keys to the bathroom. The tickets for a greasy box lunch, for the dining car that opens briefly, serves each class at separate times.

Eating: At the stops, a moment to jump off, buy peanuts from the vendors who swarm up. Candy, sometimes oranges or steamed *baozi*. Beijing to Hu He Hao Te in mid-June, the weather too hot for food, fans turning, windows open even though the soot blows in. Everybody stacked along one aisle of windows, watching. There it is—the winding shadow in the twilight. The Great Wall.

I get off once in Inner Mongolia, just at dawn, the station a line of cold shadows against a wash of rose. Then the miles of beige-pink clay homes, looking hand molded, as if the thumb print could still be traced on the chimneys, on the rounded walls that make a courtyard in the front, pigs in the yard, a chicken on a window sill. Slant roofs, and the whole front of each home a maze of tiny windows, broken by leaded patterns or wooden carved designs, intricately painted, sometimes colored paper across the panes—more like living in a flowered trellis than a house.

Hard Sleeper: Late night boarding out of Tianjin, twenty-two hours to Shanghai. I have my ticket, but the slip of paper with the number of my bunk's been lost. I have to wait through four stops till every bunk is filled except one, then scramble up just before the attendants turn the lights off. We rock in sleep until the music starts, waking the long open car of bunks, stacked three to the ceiling. Hard sleeper's mostly men and local. I'm the only foreign face. Everybody's friendly, everybody finally gives up on my limited Chinese. Halfway to Shanghai, one man reveals he knows some English, and everybody laughs about how long it took him to own up. Still, we don't converse—too much of an effort, too shy, each a bit ashamed of our poor skills. I don't mind; I like the solitude that language barriers grant me.

The men hang their tiny washcloths neatly on the curtain rod, roll them up like blinds to watch the view. I think I can't get clean here anyway, so I go dirty. We sit on the bunks or on tiny wooden seats unlatched from the wall, a single line in the aisle beside hinged tables, with the thermoses below. Attendants slosh past with battered pots of boiling water. Passengers provide their own cups, tea leaves, and noodles. Sometimes the attendants mop up the peanut shells and the watermelon seeds spit on the floor.

We could be traveling to a prison camp—the same sense of being herded together in a cramped unprivate space, the toilet flooding with piss, the boredom, the fog of cigarettes, the men with bags of seeds and fruit and chicken, the door left constantly open in December. A studious type with hair half-falling into his glasses bursts occasionally into bits of opera.

Now the music from the speakers comes more gently, a flute and the slow-plucked Chinese strings. I look out the window into the typical stretches of empty fields—hard to believe that eighty percent of the population lives in the countryside. I see one man, walking with baskets hung from poles across his shoulders. Miles later, another, cycling easily down a dirt path as if he heard the rhythms piped inside the train. I'm half asleep and peaceful, wrapped in this landscape of song, the China that I dreamed I'd come to.

The Sheet: My first time in a hard sleeper, I find the bunk made up with a bottom sheet, a pillow with a towel across it (just a northern custom, not actually meant for washing), the blanket folded at the foot. No top sheet. I accept this. In the morning, I see men fold up top sheets. I accept this too. Nothing is standard. Hours later, the train attendant comes by, tidying up. He wants my folded top sheet. *"Mei you,"* I say, "not have." And regret my lack of tenses in Chinese verbs. Last night, not have. Today, not have. His smile says he doesn't believe me. He's waiting for my sheet. The other train attendants get involved. The Chinese passengers who've ridden with me all these hours conduct a helpful search. No sheet. Things begin to get ugly. The attendants want money for this sheet I've never slept in, never seen. I consult my dictionary for words. I enlist the one man who speaks some English. I'm ready to pull foreign rank, to say I live in the Jin Jiang Hotel in Shanghai, a grand hotel with sheets changed every week, why would I steal one from a train? And suddenly a man has found it, a small folded heap half-buried beneath the bottom bunk, knocked there somehow long before I climbed up to the top one last night. The passengers start laughing at this good end to the problem, laughing in a way that makes me finally understand how differently they've seen the matter. Not a simple, silly problem, a complication in the language and a slightly harrassed foreigner. But something real, something out of place, something you'd have to pay for.

WUXI MUSIC

Outside the city of Wuxi lies Tai Hu, a wide lake hemmed by low hills in the distance, behind the sails of junks. A lyrical stretch of fish ponds, webbed with small hand-molded dikes, winds off for miles from the lake's edge. We follow the narrow dirt path along the tops of dikes, crossing little arched bridges. Sunset tints the ponds and air as rose and silver as the pale notes of a flute; we seem to walk inside a song, feeling it brush our skin, breathing its pastel tones. Kingfishers flash blue-green in twilight; when the real night falls, white geese become dim lamps, craning their necks around the edge of sheds, honking us past.

Midnight, drifting through the hotel's gardens, we find an old swimming pool built into the lake's shore. At one end, a small pagoda, at the other a stone bathhouse with curved eaves and portals, intricately grand as a tiny Taj Mahal, surreal in the dark moon shadows, the rising lake mist. We stand a long time on the pond's far edge, with the waves at our feet shifting against the tiles and the silent memory of exotic strings, bowed rich and royal, rising from this carved elegance of silhouettes.

And morning comes, sunny with breakfast and bedlam, with watching the butcher, the baker, the candlestick maker—the waiters and cooks in their white hotel clothes and puffed caps, stuffed into a rowboat the size of a tub. They slip between houses on high wooden stilts, disappear beneath buildings and backpaddle out—their laughter and antics as constant and silly as rhythms in nursery book rhymes.

BEIJING MEN

Winter's the appropriate season for Beijing. The countryside lies bleak and brown and flat as North Dakota, with bound shocks of corn intertwined to make snow fences. The bare trees, frozen rivers, and moats match the stern austerity of the city with its broad avenues—the planned grandeur of Washington, DC, the sense of its own self-importance, like any capital. The rules begin here and lose momentum as they travel south and west, become less strictly enforced. Drivers here use real headlights at night, hardly ever hit their horns; people watch the traffic signals, spill less randomly into the streets—less of the racket and ramshackle *joie de vivre* of Shanghai. The straight lines of solid brick suit the capital and the cold.

Heat's allowed here, necessary in the often sub-zero days. Heavy black padded plastic hangs across the doors to hold the warmth inside. The soot from coal stoves stings my eyes; I often walk with tears streaming down my face. The sun rises in the smog and smoke; quiet figures bike to work beside me.

The great sweeping changes that characterize the shifts of government in China's history happened here. Hard to imagine Kubla Khan now. But from one hill in a park I can watch it all—the gold-tiled roofs of the emperors' palace, the broad-

91

avenued present, the future rising in skyscrapers, freeways, and factories spewing fumes that mix with coal soot.

This is the city of diplomats and opera, the place I'd have chosen, if the Ministry of Education had asked me where I'd like to teach. My swollen eyes thank them for not having given me the option. It would have been as dangerous for my heart as for my eyes. The Beijing men attract me as most Shanghainese do not.

Two varieties of men here. The short ones cause me no problem. Heavy-set, heavy-jowled, with stubble like the fields' wheat sheaves on fat chins, broad peasant faces. The furred earflaps on their green caps stick out perpendicular to their cheeks when they ride past on a bike, or sidesaddle on a cart pulled by an equally big-boned horse. They match the stolid mountains, stubbled in winter like jaws. Earth-bound, a diet of potatoes and hot joints of meat. I'm sure their hearts beat friendly and big-bellied as their laughter, but I've always been neurotic about my own weight, and demanded the same famished silhouette in lovers.

So I find my danger in the tall, high-cheekboned slim ones, with their padded army-green greatcoats slung casually around their shoulders, not really worn, only carried with style. They boarded the plane with me, out of Shanghai; they walk here in the streets.

And sometimes in the paths of the Forbidden City, where the grandest carved and jeweled throne sits in the most intimate chamber. I sit in the garden, beneath the two gnarled cypresses that intertwine beyond all parting, listening to the plucked strings of a *pipa*. A young version of the tall men stands by the dragon pagoda; an older, more sinister one in a greatcoat and fur hat stands to his left. I smile at both; their eyes follow me as I leave the Forbidden City's gate, climb the steep stairs to the pavilion on the hill behind it. Beijing stretches everywhere below me, as the sun sets surreally red into the frozen smog.

The handsomely sinister man shows up on my hill, and at

the bus stop below it. But when I consult my map and find I have to switch directions, to wait on the opposite side of the street for a bus, the man becomes a lonely figure, unable to cross now with any dignity, stranded and a little silly, as the passing buses cover and then reveal him, still standing there.

I make my way back to the heart of foreign life in this city, the Beijing Hotel, where some Syrian man sits down at my table—to discuss the latest racial trouble with the foreign students at Tongji University in Shanghai. He has a friend who joins us, the attaché for the Syrian embassy. The attaché is short and ugly, diplomatically sleazy, inviting me to come home with him, no strings attached, to the embassy splendor of his apartment.

But I prefer the icy wait on the avenue, for a bus that drops me near my cheap hotel. I push through the black heavy plastic, past the courtyard to the bath, where the rules for hot water never match my schedule, and back again to my room, that opens on the lobby that will be noisy again by dawn.

I dream I ride a bus and watch a truck pass the window. In the middle of its bed of Chinese cabbage sits a tall man, with his green, fur-collared greatcoat tossed around his shoulders. He holds his head high, like his cheekbones, reclines there in a casual dignity my bus can never catch.

AGNES SMEDLEY AND ME

J ust inside the doors to the Museum of Chinese History in
Beijing, I'm standing before the glass sales counter, filled
with terra cotta replicas. I want to buy the tiny one called
"The Storyteller"—an old woman with fallen breasts, sitting with one foot thrust out in a good kick, one arm waving
a flat stick, a drum crooked in the other, and the widest grin
I've seen in China. But the young saleswoman is busy, and
ten classes of Chinese schoolchildren are entering the museum,
so I race ahead to beat them through the exhibition.

Later, I circle back to the counter, find the museum's interpreter talking with the saleswoman. A round young man in
a black suit, he seizes me politely. This happens often. All the
Chinese want a chance to check their English with a native
speaker. My friend Antoinette was even accosted while climbing the thousands of steps up Mt. Huangshan—"Hello? You
speak English? I have a question." And out comes the book
and the underlined sentences that don't compute inside a second language learner. The interpreter has no book, only a
copy of the words to the song "Five-Hundred Miles," typed
neatly in the most formal of English: "Lord, I am one, Lord, I
am two...." I turn the "I am's" to contractions, explain that
"this way" should be "thisa way," a kind of filler thrown in
to move the beat along, like the Chinese fill a pause with "*ne*

94

ge, ne ge," when they're talking. "Not a shirt on my back" doesn't mean the singer's naked, only broke.

It's mid-December. The interpreter thinks that people in the U.S. sing this song at Christmas. He looks a little crest-fallen when I gently correct him. But he wants to help me now, so I ask him about the exhibit next door, and I let him help me buy the terra cotta figure, though my Chinese skills can handle the transaction. According to the saleswoman, the figures cost only three *kuai,* so I buy two and head off with my bargain.

Nothing is easy to enter in China. To get to the second museum which shares this building, I have to go outside to the street, purchase another ticket, and re-enter. I'm lucky today because someone leads me through the maze of rooms to the special exhibit on Anna Louise Strong, Agnes Smedley, and Edgar Snow, billed as "The Three American Friends of China." Strong looks lovely, aging in the photos from chic radical to round, curly headed grandmother without the grandchildren. Smedley's serious in fatigues, Snow as dashing as some twenties' British white hunter. What a China they lived! They inspire me, and I'm chastised to think I'm less big hearted and good willed about this country than they were. But it was a different country then, and they lived at the center of its marching vision. I console myself by remembering it's more difficult to get excited about the Four Modernizations.

It's harder to console myself about the photos. Snow with his smiling wife, Snow with his children, Snow in his jodhpurs. Perfect as the cover of a movie star magazine. Yes, the dashing men can have both adventure and romance, but the women have to choose. Why doesn't Smedley have a handsome husband, smiling support at her elbow? None of these sturdy, solemn Chinese men beside her in their army dress quite fills the role. And Strong in her grandmotherly smock and pants is laughing at her birthday cake, held not in the arms of family, but of several Chinese friends. These women weren't alone, but they were alone in a way that Snow wasn't.

95

They traded something for that different family of friends and peasant soldiers and smiling Chinese babies. Snow didn't. Or perhaps they didn't trade. Maybe it wasn't a conscious matter of trading. The choice was made for them: be adventurous or be a woman.

In the midst of my ruminations, two women stop me—the saleswoman from the other museum and a semi-bilingual visitor who translates. They maintain that the interpreter gave me the wrong price for the statues I bought, that the price was too low. We're so sorry you had to pay so much, they say. You mean, I answer, you're so sorry you had to track me down through all these rooms to make me pay some more. I'm angry that they've gone on this bloodhound hunt and angry with myself for being angry. What would Agnes Smedley have done? Paid the extra *kuai* and smiled?

This also happens often in China—the price increases after the waiter has poured the wine and everyone believes I'd have ordered it anyway, whatever the cost. "Foreigner" is supposed to be a synonym for "wealth." The women offer to bring the interpreter but show up again, minutes later, without him. My train for Tianjin leaves soon; I can't stay to argue, and by this time I've Agnes Smedley'ed myself into paying the difference. I hand over the money just as the interpreter arrives, completely flustered. It seems that as soon as I left the counter, the saleswoman called his director and said he'd given me the wrong price. Some vendetta toward him perhaps, or she'd made a mistake and quickly moved to place the blame on someone else. That's common too in China, but knowing that does nothing for the poor interpreter who's begging me now: "You speak some Chinese. Tell her yourself that it was she who gave the wrong price." I do. She understands, a bit unwillingly. Maybe the director will understand too.

But what if I had left the museum without going to the "three friends" exhibition? If I had been big hearted, paid up on the spot before my anger stalled us long enough to let the young interpreter arrive? In Smedley's China, the right gesture was a generous one, without a hesitation. In my China, maybe justice comes sometimes because I choose to wait and to protest. The adventurous woman—another name for bitch. At least, I've made my own choice of the role. It's time to catch my train for Tianjin.

XIA YU

Raining again. Even the words sound like falling drops, *xia yu, xia yu*. The Shanghai sky hangs like soiled wet cotton, the grey more persistent even than winters at home in the Northwest, where we give the fern-choked forest the name of rain. Only here, even grass can't grow, the earth's too full of clay and constant feet. Over Suzhou Creek, the clouds turn slowly darker than the wooden barges, darker than the water's mud.

The wrong time to take the bus. Nobody getting off and twenty people waiting to crowd on. From a shop across the street, we listen to an old U.S. pop tune, backed now with a Hong Kong disco beat, Chinese and English lyrics alternating in the verses: "Tell Laura I love her, tell Laura not to cry." Like high schoolers in the 1950s, the Chinese thrive on innocent romance.

When the bus arrives, the accordion doors somehow fold us all inside. The ticket seller is thinner than her regulation jacket, wears her hair like the Laura in that 50s tune must have. She furls the five stars back into her red flag and starts her own song: "Please buy your ticket. Shaanxi Lu, the next stop." I know the routine though I can't understand her Shanghai dialect, let it fall familiar on my shoulders, the syllables of her voice like late afternoon rain.

I also know the cost of a ticket for my destination, hand

her one *mao*, with a nod to indicate I've got the fare right, so she doesn't have to try to read my version of her language. She smiles. She takes away my wet umbrella that's pressing against me in the crowd, hangs it on the rail beside her counter. I feel like something's passed between us, gently trustful as a high school ring.

CHRISTMAS IN HANGZHOU

Our Chinese friends are fond of repeating pithy sayings, some age-old bit of wisdom summed up in a line or two. They also like advising us on where to travel, to find what they call "beauty spots." These two pleasures come together in their favorite saying—"Above, there is heaven, below, there are Hangzhou and Suzhou."

We've all tried Suzhou, just over an hour's train ride from Shanghai; we've walked the charming back streets beside canals that web the old part of the city; we've drunk tea in the many gardens. We agree that Suzhou's lovely, but Hangzhou comes much closer to our foreigner's dream of heaven. Not the city itself, which resembles other Chinese cities, concrete and shabby, crowded. It's the lake we love, criss-crossed with causeways of delicate arched bridges and pagodas, and the woods around the lake, rising into hills of bamboo forest and tea. And overlooking the lake, the Hangzhou Hotel, the very heart of heaven.

This is no ordinary hotel, but a joint-venture with Hong Kong, which means the rooms are as clean and gracious as the lobby, unlike the Chinese habit of letting marble and pillared entries fade off quickly into peeling walls and cockroaches. It means that the bathrooms come with phones and music, with bubble bath in packets, with towels, toilet paper, and reliable hot water. It means that when the Hong Kong management's on duty, the waitresses in the restaurant smile, the meal comes quickly, and it's what we ordered. And what trouble we take, trying to choose between the possible delights: pizza and real cheeses, the famous apple strudel, the Irish coffees—things unavailable in Shanghai. We have the menu memorized, with annotations covering what's predictably successful, and what can sometimes come too cold or salty. We understand that true perfection is a dream, like heaven; we understand that this is merely Hangzhou, a joint-venture, with half its roots in China. Still, it's dream enough, and like world-weary souls who long to rest in paradise, we talk on Shanghai buses, jammed between the dust and spitters, about Hangzhou, about sleeping in the hotel's firm, fresh beds, the coverlet turned down each night by angels, knocking softly for room service.

Although the hotel's grand by even Western standards, by those same standards the rates are cheap, and still too costly to allow us frequent pilgrimages on our Chinese salaries. But traditionally, Westerners go into debt at Christmas, and so we go to Hangzhou.

Chinese trains are never late, but Christmas morning dawns so thick with fog that this last efficiency breaks down. We wait three hours in the cold station, then our train creeps into Hangzhou, where our cab sits trapped between the cars and trolleys for so long that even the driver begins to swear and we laugh, recognizing the words, a solid percentage of our tiny Mandarin vocabularies. At last, the cab is pulling up the hotel's circle drive, past a group of hostesses walking to their shift in Suzie Wong gowns with long grey winter underwear peeking out beneath the skirts' slits. Here's another hostess at the door to greet us—Doris, our favorite—and our favorite porter, a young man who in private we call Kentucky, because he speaks English with a drawl. All the service people have been given English first names by the Hong Kong management, chosen for alliteration with their Chinese family name. So a waitress may be Wendy Wong. Kentucky's hotel name is Chopin Chu, perhaps explaining why his English sounds so musical.

It's already four o'clock, too close to dinner time to eat, but as soon as we're checked in, we hit the restaurant for the hotel's special cheese plate and some beer. The pencil-thin young manager we call the Hong Kong man is here, smiling, lighting our cigarettes, spreading a joy more soothing than an angel's harp. The luckier friends who came here yesterday appear and, while the sun sets, we stroll the bit of land that juts out in the lake, like a semi-attached island, lined with benches and vaguely Victorian street lamps. We've signed up for the hotel's Christmas feast; we're trying to walk off the cheese plates.

And now we dress for dinner. Everyone has brought some clothes besides our usual jeans or sweatpants, something delicate, something we wear only when we know we're not taking buses, not dining in a place that drenches everything in rapeseed oil. We gather on big chairs and couches in the lobby beside the fountain, where an only slightly garish symphony of colored lights plays through the falling waters. We indulge in cocktails, spicy little crackers, and peanuts. We're leisurely, knowing this is not a state-run restaurant, so the kitchen won't shut down at six or even seven.

We drift up to our table, and the night's five courses begin to arrive, Western style, one after the other, not randomly or all at once, the way a Chinese banquet sometimes happens. Here's wine and a duck paté, presented beside a fluted radish. And here's the Hong Kong man. It seems there's not quite enough turkey and wouldn't we like a bit of ham included in the main course then? We're amazed he hasn't just walked up, announcing *"mei you,"* "not have." We're sure that we're in paradise. And sure that all the preachers have been wrong about gluttony; it's clearly not a sin, but one of the rewards of heaven.

The next morning we wake to quiet mist above the lake, clinging to the trees and temples, to the small pagoda just below the window, and the delicate plucked strings of *pitang* music, drifting through our rooms at the touch of a button. We wake to tea and breakfast decisions, to a slow walk up the backstreets where a child in padded winter layers bursts into tears, frightened by the foreign faces, and still so like my own child self, wrapped up in my thick red snowsuit. Steep stairs lead us to the ridge behind the hotel, where three Chinese women sit in a sort of tiny temple, built for taking in the view. One sings, trying out her bits of English song, the words slipping past her crooked forward teeth and the gaps around them. We pass the old men taking their birds for a stroll, hanging their square, blue-covered wooden cages in the trees. Pet birds, that cost a month of Chinese salary. Pet birds, forbidden in the Cultural Revolution, treasured now.

The hill of bamboo forest descends to Chinese reconstruction, to the bamboo weave of temporary housing for the workers, everybody coming home with a fish or chicken for dinner, unmarked holes in the streets—an easy misstep into the buried sewer. Bicycles thread the lake's mist. Men row long wooden boats across it, with canopies against the rain that never came today. They head for the middle island, with its four reflecting ponds designed to catch the moon that's rising now as we pack bags and gather in the lobby, Christmas over, time for cabs. We're sad as exiles out of heaven should be, wanting to hug the smiling angels, the Hong Kong man's thin shoulders, Doris in her tight slit dress at the door, the last Kentucky drawl "goodby."

And the cab's unloading at the station, with its usual masses of travelers, waiting, sitting on their heaps of red and blue and white striped plastic baggage, ready to fight for the train, to climb in its windows to ensure a seat. Carl or Paul or someone sighs, "Back in the Third World again," the way all exiles talk, all cynical and resigned, when they leave paradise. Next Christmas, we'll be scattered—in New York, in Paris, in Quebec's small Rivière du Loup, Seattle, Sydney, some tiny town along the coast of Spain. Those places will by then seem no more heavenly than usual. We'll bore our friends with pithy sayings that we know mean nothing to them, mean something only to the distant friends who open letters and remember how the heavens up above don't matter, glad the earth is wound with airmail flights that take us back to wisdom, back to Christmas in the Hangzhou Hotel, when we understood how simple wants fulfilled meant simply heaven.

CHINESE POSING

Not a derogatory term. Not indicating artificial manners or deception. Merely the name the foreigners have given to a favorite local pastime, to the fixation on cameras and the studied postures people take before them.

If the Chinese go on holiday, they come back loaded with photos, but a viewer could never guess they'd traveled more than ten steps from their homes. Here's Wang, and Wang again, and another smiling likeness—and whatever monument or mountain peak she's posed beside is mostly lost outside the frame.

And what poses! Holding up her hands to catch the sun's beam, or draping a slim branch of willow across her smile, the leaves tangling in her black hair.

Walking down the Shanghai waterfront, I have to remind myself that China's sexuality lies mostly in the realm of "Father Knows Best" or Ward and June Cleaver. For here are young men with cameras, and young women posing, stretched full-length on the concrete railing, with their heads thrown back, and their skirts hitched up a bit, odalisques in white blouses and anklets.

Kitsch is also part of this—posing on the mangy camel outside the yurts in Hu He Hao Te or the inevitable Mongolian white pony. Enterprise belongs here too. Photographers at tourist sites rent costumes—ancient silk robes, capes, and sabers. At Louyang, the Buddhist carvings cover miles of cliffs beside the river, some tiny as a thumb, some two stories tall. Signs prohibit photos. But everyone ignores this. And businesses spring up beside the tallest saints. A young woman at a table in the spring's heat collects the money for the cameraman. But I snap her instead, demure in her white transparent gloves with a grandmother's button at the wrist, pink ribbons on her floppy broad-brimmed hat.

Peggy and I travel to Xi'an, famous in the West for its buried fields of terra cotta warriors ranged around an emperor's tomb, life-sized, life-like replicas discovered when some peasants tried to dig a well. For us, Xi'an is famous for its street food—for dumplings dipped in communal basins of red chile sauce, for the salty marinated beef in pocket-shaped bread. And famous for its shopping. We call it *"mai dongxi,"* the "buy things" city. One morning, we spend hours in a tiny shop, the shelves stuffed with everything from ancient scholar's caps—child-sized, with a fake braid trailing from the red-tasseled black silk—to antique chains with silver implements for cleaning fingernails and ears. We bargain, laughing, with the old man there, and then we ask to take his picture. Certainly, he agrees, and pulls out a self-addressed envelope for a copy, pulls out an album of himself with countless other tourists. And now I'm there in Kodak gloss beside his big smile, shiny in my royal blue nylon poncho.

But I never learn the art of Chinese posing, stay self-conscious before the lens, shy as the girls selling vegetables in the market and, like them, still secretly wanting the attention. Sometimes at lunch Suzanne and I try to catch the eye of our school's photographer, a handsome man who stands around the dining hall with easy poise and class, his gear slung about his shoulders, wearing casual cotton shirts and pants, his feet in sandals. The quintessential journalist. He never took our picture.

When I return home, the West takes over, and I forget about Chinese posing. Then one night I go with visitors from Chongqing to see the Christmas ships, their colored lights like jewels strung in the bay. The choir on board sings carols, and look, I say, there's Santa Claus. But the visitors are busy with their cameras, posing over and over for the snapshots that I know will tell the relatives back home so little, tell them only that their friends were smiling, though the night was cold beyond their bundled parkas, and something in the corner of the frame glowed.

THE WORD THE MEN DON'T KNOW

Wu Zetian challenged feudal concepts by assuming the title Hu-angdi, *a term which can only be properly translated as emperor. A woman involved in political affairs was likened to "a hen reporting the dawn..."*

"History's Only 'Daughter of Heaven'"—Chu Nan

Like women everywhere, women in China hold up most of the sky, receive lip-service recognition for half of it, and little tangible thanks. Super moms, working the double day. The great leaps of Liberation seem to have slowed down to steps that cover distances as small as bound feet, sometimes just a stepping in place.

The big picture looks good from a distance: women in what the West would term traditionally male fields, women in the news, some journals devoted wholly to their status and achievements. Look closer now and check how few manage factories, sit in the Great Hall of the People or on the Party's Central Committee.

I interview Dai Hou Ying, a controversial Shanghai novelist. We discuss the recent International PEN conference in New York, where feminist writers protested the lack of women on conference panels, and Norman Mailer defended the composition of the panels by claiming that most male writers were intellectuals first and most females were not. No Chinese man, notes Dai, would be so foolish as to say such things out loud—instead, the men speak correctly, but when they send a delegation somewhere, they send few, if any, women.

Two female students sit in my office, discussing feminist writers. I suggest that women in China need to unite, to pass some laws in their favor. My students remind me that nobody passes laws in China. "OK, then you need women on the Central Committee." My students giggle, overcome by my silliness. Then they switch the focus. Many women remain unenlightened, they say. "So educate them." Yes, they respond, our women writers are trying that. Then they ask me, "Dr. James, what do you think is the meaning of life?"

As part of the one-child family campaign, the government's trying to upgrade women, to make a daughter seem as satisfying as a son. One billboard illustrates improper behavior by picturing a grandma cuddling a baby boy, ignoring the outstretched arms of a girl. It's one step toward enlightenment.

Still, in class, most students, male and female, maintain that men are stronger than women. I make my usual argument, reminding them of the old women who pull heavy carts while the men sit around card tables, smoking. I back up my point with exaggerated pantomime and win a laugh, but not the battle. I discuss the same issue often with my writer friend, a man in his seventies. We argue genially, with Ming translating. We agree to disagree. But really, aren't women softer, Ming asks—what about Adam and Eve? That, I tell her, is a story made up by a man. Those "soft" old women pull their carts, and smoke tough cigarettes in public, with all the arrogance that a long march grants them. My young Chinese friends just sneak cigarettes in my room, women's night out. Often my female students remind me of their counterparts in the States—so many seem co-opted back into the stereotypes of femininity, thinking the struggle's won or can't be. I feel like the tough old vanguard of the march, wondering how to pass on the flags.

109

Certainly women are safer here than back home. But I suspect this safety stems from the general lack of violence on Chinese streets, not from some chivalrous concern. And the violence is likely to increase with the coming of capitalism. Now, however, Ming and I talk fearlessly on a late night corner. When a man on a bike rides up and suddenly touches Ming's arm, my Western instincts revive; I get ready to burn him with my cigarette. But he's stopped only because he heard her excellent English; he's telling her about a job in the States. Walking home alone one night, I sing an Aretha Franklin tune; a man begins to set his pace to mine. I cross the street; he doesn't. I realize he was simply listening to my Western blues, like tracking the Voice of America on mobile shortwave.

While Qiang Qing's the modern image of the ruthless woman, Wu Zetian's the ancient story. Shifted from royal concubine to nun and back to concubine, Wu Zetian seized control of her fortunes, rose through a maze of bloody intrigues to rule the country. The legend says she told one emperor that she could tame his wild horse. First, she said, she'd use an iron whip; if the horse refused to obey, she'd beat it with a hammer; if it still refused, she'd cut its throat. With legends like that, it's men who might not feel safe on the streets, might be spreading the rumor of female weakness out of self defense.

Or take the old opera of a woman forced to marry a short, ugly man she finds repellent. She falls in love with his brother, who sacrifices their mutual passion by leaving the city as a good hero must. So the woman drops into the less grandly virtuous arms of another lover, and the two of them kill her husband so she can escape. Traditionally, of course, she's been cast as a villain. Now a director stages the opera new, adding female characters from Chinese fiction, some modern real-life women, and Anna Karenina. They appear at intervals to discuss the plot and the status of women. At the end they stage a trial to determine who's really been the victim.

Still, Mr. Han's wife is in the kitchen when we come to

lunch, and stays there while we eat, and nothing can bring her out for more than a brief appearance behind the steaming dishes.

Some feet keep taking steps, however small. Young women friends chatter beside me about feminism, using the English word in their Chinese sentences. There is a Chinese word for feminism, they assure me, but the men don't know it. Perhaps the whole country will wake up to it one morning, when the hen reports the dawn.

WELCOME TO HAVE A TRY

I'm a fool for words. I make a dangerous teacher of English—because I love creative mistakes. Today, a friend from home writes, lamenting her students' lack of language skills. One boy turned in an essay about *Death of a Salesman*, describing Willy Loman as "a guy who didn't have a lot of wins." Sometimes you have to break the grammar rules to tell the truth.

Mistakes can charm. There's always charm in Chinglish— what everyone, both foreign and Chinese, calls the pidgin language spoken here. Before the opera starts, my Chinese lover tries to summarize the setting and the plot. "This country," he says charmingly, "is living in a desert." If I do something particularly well, he says I give him a deep impression. If I make him sad, he says, "You kill my heart." English as a second language twists cliches fresh.

And creates its own stock phrases. Any lovely place one travels to is called a "beauty spot"; everything eaten on a holiday is summed up as "delicious dishes." Our favorite expression is "Welcome to have a try." So hospitable, so easily varied to fit the situation. A sign at an airport reads "Welcome to fly CAAC," the Chinese airline; at an exhibition one may be welcomed to have a look. One day big posters line my hotel lobby; they "welcome all the participants of Shanghai

Fair 86 and individual passengers to take part in our programs." I go back to my room for my camera, to photograph the descriptions of these tours, happy as an archeologist documenting pot sherds on a good dig. The trip to the Jade Pagoda promises "no matter you believe in or not, Buddha 'bless' you all the time, if you go there you will have good luck." Or try Yu Garden, where "Oriental architecture make you more outlandish as you away from your country." Outlandish perhaps as the Square Pagoda that "looks like a slim girl ware a mini-skirt, in China you can never have to see too many pagodas." But this is a business conference, after all, and so tour number ten encourages a visit to the "carpet fac. and silk fac.... if not going to the silk fac., you may regret all of your life."

Chinglish charms like poems, like anything that stands the language on its head. The humor helps us break routines: eating every night in her hotel's restaurant, Marcia grows bored with the menu, begins to order only the dishes that are misspelled.

The foreigners begin to lose words—the names of things too culture-bound to come up in a conversation here, vocabulary beyond our students' skills. What's that word for something artificial, I ask my friends, feeling its fake texture beneath my fingers, like the velvet of those paintings in Mexican restaurants, those Last Supper panoramas spread beside the road on flea-market days back home. Hours later, I say "ersatz." One night I turn my search for words into charades. I'm trying to remember the name of that fifties' television star who began her program by sweeping in through double doors, then closing them, her full skirts swirling. Halfway through the wine and several sweeping entries, some foreigner shouts "Loretta Young." Then Paul loses the name of his favorite painter at home. And he's from Canada so none of us can help him. Instead we turn his loss into a tease. For a month we punctuate our conversations randomly with sudden references: "Like that painter you described, Paul. What's his name?"

Still I keep my hold on English firm enough to keep me dangerous. I hear the difference between the short wave lies the Voice of America sends in rapid native speaker language and the lies it broadcasts in the slow thirty-three-and-a-third rhythms of its "News in Special English." Many U.S. companies, the VOA reports, are moving to the deep South. Kentucky, it says, is a right-to-work state—the Special English version of union-busting.

I'm street-wise when it comes to words, but I don't change door locks, let language, like a faithless lover, keep the key. A fool for charm, I turn the shortwave till I find the Big Ben chimes, while the Shanghai evening closes down around my room, the one bulb flickering dimly from my ceiling. And a voice says "This is London" and I'm hooked.

True Stories

This is a true story. A foreign teacher in Shanghai was
ill for some weeks and went several times to a local clinic.
Each time she was treated by the same two young male
doctors. On her last visit, they asked if she would explain
some words they had been unable to find in their English-
Chinese dictionaries. They gave her a large sheet of paper
with the words *tampax, marijuana, cunnilingus, wow.*

This is a true story. The woman had been teaching in China
for a long time. She was good at explaining delicate matters.
She took the paper and drew a picture of a tampax, then described what women did with it and why. The men listened,
frowning: "They put THAT there?" The picture was very large.
"Well," she said, "in real life, it is smaller." The doctors re-
laxed.

Next she explained marijuana. That was easy. Doctors
understand drugs. Chinese medicine is full of plants and
powders gathered at odd times under a certain moon. And
Westerners have strange habits—they like to make themselves
crazy with drugs as well as cured.

Time for cunnilingus. Very carefully, very clinically, she began
her definition. Halfway through, the doctors' cheeks turned
like a hot day at the beach. They covered their ears. They ran.

She never got to wow.

THE EIGHT-PENIS FISH

Suzanne and I have spent the day traipsing through the streets of Kunming, trying to find the place that sells tickets to Dali, a tiny city about ten hours away by bus. At least Kunming lies in the south of China, so the February weather's warm. The tailors cut their cloth bolts in the sun, and even the white-capped medics are out, sitting at tables by street corners, ready to check heartbeats, part of the latest campaign for health.

At dinner, we run into Shanghai friends just back from Hong Kong, full of the wonders of cheap high-fashion and Italian restaurants. We haven't been to Hong Kong yet, and find the fresh green snowpeas miracle enough, after weeks of cabbage. We drink too much of the local beer, and still we have to set our clocks for five a.m. to catch the Dali bus.

I wake. I fill a shallow bath, saving the last hot water for Suzanne. By the time I'm lacing up my shoes, I'm angry because Suzanne's still sleeping and I'm sure we'll miss the bus. Suddenly she wakes, staring first at me, and then at the clock I haven't bothered to consult. It's only two. I go back to bed, feeling silly but so cleanly warm. And later, that becomes the day's first gift, because at five the water's cold.

Tearing handfuls of breakfast from our plastic bag of bread, we haul our luggage up the dark street now, into the mini-

116

van that the day's long roads will teach us has no suspension. Three other foreigners jam in and we're surprised to find they're friends we met in Guilin, earlier on our trip.

The road climbs into sunrise, into hills, then mountains where pine trees mix with eucalyptus, cactus, and palm. The landscape rolls out like plush velvet, yellow, green, and red. We look down into a valley, fields ribbed with water ditches, stone homes with carved wooden gates and doors. A river winds beside us, brown with soil.

Still, even in such beauty, ten hours makes a long ride in a packed van. We fill the miles with word games. "I'm thinking of a person whose name begins with T." "Were you a writer?" "No, I'm not William Thackeray." "Did you live in ancient times?" "No, I'm not King Tut." The answers become more difficult as the focus of the questions narrows. Whenever it's my turn to pick a name, I choose a woman, and we get frustrated, realizing how few names of famous women we know. The game goes on and on like the road. We'll remember this bit of river as "q," Nick says, this mountain curve as "f." Everyone plays except Cassandra who's from Hong Kong, not native in the mother tongue that binds our mix of England, Australia, and the States, and the heritage of names we share.

Almost into Dali, we're tired of alphabets and turn to jokes. Cassandra starts one. Some soldiers had to cross a river, she says, where there lived an eight-penis fish. The laughter stops her, everyone delighted by this image of a fish. Cassandra's bewildered. She knows her joke is funny, but the punch line's coming later. Well, she goes on, smiling, that's the problem— how to cross the river before the fish can eat their penises. A fish who ate penises? Yes, of course, an ate-penis fish. And all the other names for this landscape desert our native speaker tongues.

The Real Thing

It's the Coca Cola Cafe, where the skinny waitress likes to practice English, discos every night beside the ghettoblaster to her Hong Kong tapes. We're eating breakfast—sugared scrambled eggs with rich tomatoes—when the drums and gongs start, and we leave our plates to watch the Chinese New Year's Day parade. A line of men and boys comes by in navy track suits, carrying the spangled dragon head, the endless velvet body supported on tall sticks, and then the tail. The marchers move slowly, stopping to whirl the sticks until the dragon undulates in long waves.

Nick's professional, switching lenses and the zoom. I'm not, snapping anything, watching so long the breakfast plates are gone when I return. That's morning. And no one can tell us what comes next. No one seems sure. We live on rumors.

The Dali streets fill up with people buying and eating. We walk the city, gate to gate. February, but the sun is June. We eat frozen bars of rice and water on a stick. Eat pickled greens with *dofu* from a street stand, try not to watch the slipshod way the woman washes up the bowls. And still some hunger drives us back to the Coca Cola, the center of this tiny grey-stoned city. Just as we order, the drums begin—the big parade.

The thin, wild-eyed man, with a cigarette between his nearly toothless gums, must be in charge. He holds a scepter, poses for me in his pink robe, then puts on a huge pink ceramic baby's head. He leads the dance. Two men follow in the lion's body, big-eyed, big-mouthed, a laughing red mane. One woman is a butterfly with gossamer wings; one's a crane. Another wears a long robe, walking inside the paper boat she carries. In Dali, women blossom always into color, wear side-buttoned tunics, blue and burgundy, with white, embroidered sleeves and aprons, some with their braids wound up in yarn or flowered towels wrapped fast with safety pins. Now five of them go by like that, their mirrored sunglasses exotic in this place. Behind them, men carry leafy branches, play gongs and cymbals, more drums.

Nick's left me, and Cassandra, and Suzanne. Gone back to cooling rice inside the Coca Cola. But I can never get enough of holidays. I follow the parade until it stops before a red-bannered store, and the crowd throws strings of fireworks. The lion makes his dancing leaps to bless the shop; the leopard boys turn cartwheels. The women dance, tapping wooden finger cymbals and sticks. One bumps me; when I say *mei-guanxi*, "no problem," she turns giddy at my foreigner's Chinese, and they all laugh, crowding beside me. This is the day's big show. The robed woman sings to the dipping rhythms of her paper boat, men beside her, paddling, swaying their branches. The butterfly and crane dance; the magician chants.

So the cafe's named the Coca Cola. So the flowers in the dancers' hair are plastic, the diamonds only sparkling tinsel on their clothes. So what. It's one more new year in this city of a thousand old ones. Everything's rhinestone and real. The illusion holds.

CHINA'S CHINATOWN

It's hard to say whether Guangzhou (known so long in the West as Canton) is the future of China or its past. Certain touches I associate with an older China—the lanterns, the red and gold decor on shop fronts—things that have disappeared from other cities linger here. Guangzhou's what any North American would recognize as Chinatown, that section of San Francisco or Vancouver, Canada—swollen now to hold the entire city and transplanted back to its home. Most of the Chinese who emigrated west came from these southern regions and left enough years ago to carry with them a China that hardly exists in China now.

Foreign capitalists were part of that Chinese past, and Guangzhou has long been famous as a city for doing business. My Shanghai friends say the Shanghainese were sharper business people, but the ones from Guangzhou banded together, formed associations. The Shanghainese were too individualistic to organize, so the Guangzhou businesses won out. I recognize these businessmen from my own Chinatowns at home: the suits, the mannerisms, the extra weight that signifies the over-fed middle class, their wives dressed better than other women, their voices and gestures louder—the upwardly mobile types that made it in the West.

Capitalism's also where Deng Xiao Ping, the latest helmsman, is steering the country, however obliquely—or maybe he's just hanging on while the country veers its own tiller. So the past meets future in Guangzhou.* From the revolving restaurant on the top of a tall building, I can read the city like rings on a tree's stump. The Pearl River, with people streaming over bridges, out of ferries, then the wide hem of post-Liberation reconstruction, uniformly solid and ugly, the concrete painted in peeling faded yellows and greens. In the center, the old city that's so chaotically interesting from the street, and from here looks bombed out, big holes between haphazard roofs.

I find the view depressing so I head for the street markets that cheer me anywhere in China. And I've never seen a market like this. I know the northerners traditionally looked down on the Chinese from the south, "those people who eat dogs." No dogs here, but everything else one could imagine and not imagine eating. An armadillo in a straw basket tries to escape; a boy kicks it back; it cowers, heart beating hard under its scales. A caged monkey cries more plaintively than a mating cat, bits of monkey fingers on the box beside it, dried and charcoaled black. Fishes swim or float belly up in a tank; some hang alive on a stick. On a cutting table, I see pieces that still seem to breathe. I could wear what's left like a cape, the head fitting over mine like a hood, the spine and tail flowing. I pass flat stingrays, turtles, crabs, huge prawns, needle-nosed long skinny somethings. Ducks hang with their necks twisted in an almost knot, basted to a brown lacquer. A hook through the throat holds plucked chickens, some with the wing-tip feathers left draping like the sleeves of opera robes, their yellow toes pointed and the necks tilted up in the stylized poise of stars on stage. Shoppers can buy the whole animal or a favorite part: a cow's stomach or hoof, pig's feet or snouts, the beak of a chicken or its heart.

*The economic crises that China has experienced and the political turmoil of the spring of 1989 have reminded me once again that it is foolish to make such confident predictions about China.

As the night comes on, I wander into an amusement park, brilliant with lights, two huge moving dolls and a tiger with blinking eyes, pool tables, a hall of mirrors, a ferris wheel, and bumper cars. On a small stage, would-be stars sing off-key rock and disco; with their long hair and tight pants, they manage slightly distorted copies of their Western counterparts. The typical skinniness of the country's young men looks better in this context; maybe rock stars everywhere have bodies governed by Chinese genes. Later, in the restaurant, my waitresses show an equal interest in the latest foreign fashions, hovering around my table to ask whether I want more rice, more beer, but really to discuss my earrings, the seven rings on my fingers. They be-bop when the rock tapes start and the dining room turns into a disco, with lights like a Hollywood dressing table around the band's stage, the hip kids streaming past the guards at the door.

So East meets West in Guangzhou. But which influenced which? Did the makeup on the waitresses begin with Revlon or the painted beauties on silk palace scrolls? The incredible swank of the White Swan Hotel, with its doormen and marble, its ponds of carp and open terraces rising around the inner lobby could stem from the Hyatt Regency or the Forbidden City. Just across the slim Pearl River lies Hong Kong—producer of the latest Western trends—the currents passing back and forth, impossible to separate, old and new as time.

HONG KONG MARGARITA

S low boat to Hong Kong, but the steaming air and tropi-
cal lush of trees across the muddy Pearl River seem more
like a trip up the Amazon. I've been in China so long
that the strange East seems familiar, so I reach first for the
image of some distant jungle to name this feeling—and then
the exotic sense of China comes back fresh.

A thin moon, the lights of occasional ships and homes.
Only the sound of the hull pushing forward in the quiet, then
suddenly the horn and the captain's voice coming fast and
angry, over and over, like some war movie alert. The echoes
resolve back into silence. The boat heads on, the dusky grey
silk waves rolling away from its sides in long slow folds.

We arrive just before dawn. I go out on deck, see a few
hills with scattered lamps and think it's not such a big city
after all. Then I walk to the boat's other side, and there it is,
the solid line of skyscrapers, back-lit by the rising sun. Hong
Kong.

My friend Nick, who taught here several months, swears
the one emotion in Hong Kong is greed. He's right. How easy
to be overcome by greed, where everything exists in such
profusion. A thousand neon signs on every block, oranges
lighting up the market stalls like stacked suns. I'm greedy for
the red double-decker buses, for the fast pace of the traffic

driving on the English side of the road. I'm stumbling against the horns, walking against the traffic lights, my eyes unfocused as a country bumpkin's.

It's Hong Kong, the heart of cheap high tech. So I buy some, tucking the camera into my purse to take photos of the city, and spoil the whole roll later, when the camera misfunctions and I open the cover to find the batteries that the sales clerk tossed in as an "extra bargain" were near-dead. I store my tiny new electronic typewriter in a hotel locker, safer than my dorm room bed; I remember that theft begins with possessions; I remember I'm not on the mainland, where I keep my salary in my cabinet, not bothering with a bank. I forget to buy the special typing ribbons, so the machine sits useless in my Shanghai room for months.

I'm not greedy for wristwatches, for the diamonds and furs stacked in endless windows—only for the clothes, spilling out of the shops on racks in this city that's become the heart of fashion. In the bargain shops, the clerks say, "No try on, one size fit all." All the merchandise is size nine, the most common shape in the West it gets imported to. All the clerks are size three, like myself. I understand now where the baggy styles began, the sweaters down to the knees, the coat sleeves rolled up twice. The shop girls furl the sleeves on my shirt and nod to say I look great. So I must, because I look like them and they're terrific.

I stop ten times a day to count my money, calculate the minimum I'll need for the train to the mainland, the taxi from the airport to Shanghai. I dedicate the rest to greed and buy more luggage, one of those red and blue and white striped plastic bags that Chinese carry in the PRC. My bags can barely hold my goods. I can barely lift my bags. I know tomorrow I'll suffer on the half-mile walk between the place where the Hong Kong train stops and the mainland station. I grew up Catholic in Illinois; I understand the purgatory of burning off this greedy sin. For five days, I've forgotten Marx and Lenin, now their admonitions come back in the finger-shaking shapes of childhood nuns.

I count my money one last time. Enough for dinner, and I choose Mexican, one of the many cuisines that haven't hit the streets of Shanghai. For the first and last time in my Chinese year, I order a margarita, watch it come to my table like a salted grail. My hands shake as Percival's must have. I'm afraid to pick it up, afraid I'll spill a drop of the taste of mariachi trumpets. Then I cradle it in both palms, lift it safely up to bless my lips.

ACTUAL TIME

Living on the dateline's unfamiliar side, I find the calendar
confusing. The Big Ben chimes ring morning on the shortwave as I settle into dinner. I live my day before my
friends back home wake up to theirs. They ought to call me
every morning, consult me like a horoscope.

Even inside the Chinese borders, time confuses. Everything
runs by Beijing's clock, and when we travel west to Yunnan
Province or the further world of Tibet, the dawn begins far
into morning and the sun sets long past ten.

One weekend when we've planned a trip to Xi'an, the
government decides to switch to daylight saving hours, a system not tried here before. We check the *China Daily*'s explanation to learn the details of the shift. Trains and planes, it
says, will change their schedules. They will leave, it says, at
the actual time.

V

Things Foreign

SHAKESPEARE AS YOU LIKE IT

A headline in the *China Daily*: "China presents Shakespeare as you like it." A festival of sixteen plays in Chinese. I rush to the *wai ban* (a word naming both the foreign office at my school and the Chinese who work there), begging for tickets. Which play would you like to see, Dr. James? All of them. All of them? Yes. Remember I'm your literary foreign expert.

The *wai ban*, who were billed as guardian angels before I came here, have often turned out more like guardian demons. But this time, I rag them till they make calls, even stand in line, and one day come up with several tickets. The strange translation of the bard begins.

Macbeth: Is called here *Bloody Hands*. Transformed to *kunju*, the oldest branch of Chinese opera. No witches in *kunju*, but there are roles for elves and men disguised as female clowns. So the lights go up on a witch as short as a man on his knees, and it *is* a man on his knees, in voluminous skirts that two other witches somersault from, three squat forms now, bubbling about the stage, shouting toil and trouble in Chinese, eerie and humorous at the same time. For some reason that no one can explain, a stuffed parrot has been added, talking when its obvious string is pulled. Lady Macbeth makes a perfect villain, with the stylized tight curved mouth of opera heroines and gleaming eyes. Macbeth goes mad in a frenzy. At the banquet, Banquo's ghost becomes an accusing bulk of dignity, his face painted with dramatic patterns, the lighting on them shifting from white to red and back to white. Then all the dead ones circle Lady Macbeth, with colored fire sparks shooting from their mouths. Suzanne whispers, "It's Qiang Qing," and I agree. Macbeth has long gone offstage like Mao and all the blame's laid safely on the wife. And that's the end. A Chinese viewer asks why did they give Macbeth a black beard? Heroes wear black beards and villains wear green ones. If his beard had been green, then everyone would recognize him as the villain from the start. The first Shakespearean complexity to handle.

Titus Andronicus: One of those plays one wonders why Shakespeare ever wrote. But the Chinese love a spectacle and this provides one after the other, beginning with the opening in smoky red darkness with bodies littering the steps of the stage. Hands and heads get cut off, to the grinding sound effects of saws, the sounds of gates opening before the stage hands swing them. The heroine picks up a hand with her teeth, because her own have been knifed off already. The actors do the best they can, while the spot lights roam the stage, searching for them.

Twelfth Night: Trying to find the theatre, I roam through what some foreigners call Little Xinjiang, the Shanghai district where minorities (non-Han Chinese) from Xinjiang province gather. The Han Chinese are rulers, but (with the exception of Tibet) the government sometimes treats minorities with kid gloves, especially the ones from Xinjiang, where people demonstrate sometimes against the nuclear power plants built in their province. In Little Xinjiang, residents change money on the black market and sell hash, seemingly without interference from the Hans. One man grins behind his fat cigarette; the sweet smell of dope sails past me. And the play's as sweet as that—

performed as Shaoxing opera, but in Western period costumes with some Western music. A bit of Shanghai dialect thrown in sets the audience roaring. I drift out of the theatre, as light-hearted as the grin behind a Xinjiang smoke.

Antony and Cleopatra: I meet Peggy for steamed dumplings at the Park Hotel. Our Chinese friends are fond of giving us kitschy presents, like dinner plates with kitten faces, whiskered and ribboned in the center. Today, someone has presented Peggy with a large stuffed doll. We ditch it guiltily, prop it on a chair in the hotel's public bathroom, hoping it will find its way into some local child's arms. Then we walk around the corner to a grown-up doll, a giggling, high-voiced Cleo, her arms as flabby as a matron of fifty, but the actress is only twenty-three, says a student who's come all the way from Guangzhou for the play. The men begin well, more intimacy between them than the lovers. But in the second act, Antony turns stiff, falls over after stabbing himself (not fatally yet), and his tunic flies up; he's left lying on the stage in his undershorts. Later, when he really dies, he has to stand there waiting till someone arrives to catch him when he falls. Cleo and her maid put snakes in their dresses, wriggle and shriek orgasmically.

The Taming of the Shrew: For this, they've imported a British director, now working in Hong Kong. He doesn't speak Chinese but somehow everyone manages. The play, says the *China Daily*, has some people worried because it was written "to entertain a male-dominated society in which even the ruling Queen was said to possess the heart of a man. How would contemporary Chinese audiences respond...?" I find concern like this comforting in China which, despite the advances that came with Liberation, often seems so male-dominated itself. The director unearths a modern theme in the play, the need for a balanced relation between husband and wife. He tones down the anti-female qualities, cuts the most insulting lines. "Who tames whom," he asks. "The audience will find out."

131

The audience meets other changes too, that set the play within a play, a frame of local context and humor. Petruchio becomes a Shanghai sailor, a member of the audience who complains when the cast first appears in sweat pants. I've bought tickets for Shakespeare, he shouts, storming onto the stage, where he falls into a dream, into the leading male role of the play. When he comes to tame Kate, he wears a wig, hip sunglasses, a mass of dishes hanging from his belt and the metal signs one sees on Shanghai streets that read "don't spit, don't litter." Will you take this woman to be your wife? In Chinese he answers, you're god-damned son of a bitch right. At the end, the lights go down and a voice calls give me fire, a light. Another voice reminds him those are lines from *Hamlet*. And Petruchio wakes up from his dream. Understanding Chinese not much better than the director, I can't verify the feminism of this Shakespeare, but I know that humor's part of any balance, and I'm going home laughing.

King Lear: Called *Li Ya Wang* now, the tragedy of a Chinese emperor. This production's in Beijing so I have to watch it on TV. Ignorant of science, I take photos of the best scenes, later get back endless portraits of my television. The play, says the *China Daily*, has themes pertinent to both ancient and modern China. For instance, small changes in this version highlight social justice; the king's caught in the tempest, not with a few loyal followers but among a crowd of beggars, "learning how unjust it is for some people to indulge in wanton extravagance while others are starving or freezing to death." And the play's superb. The acting, the big backdrop of a dragon set, the resilience of the actors when the set breaks and they pick up pieces while approaching Lear's bed, working the destruction into the scene. But the audience that never laughed when Antony fell over in his flying tunic snorts now, the eyes of Justice still at least aesthetically blind.

Much Ado About Nothing: A *huan mei* opera version, with the men in beautiful silk, but the women in cheap lace over tinselly gold threads, their hands forever in their sleeves so they appear like helpless dolls. I begin to see patterns in these plays, and how the Elizabethan West fits China. So often the plot makes a woman the victim of gossip, and her denials (when even made) count for nothing; the voice of a man is necessary to clear her reputation. Vocal women star as evil doers, like Lady Macbeth, or shrews (even when toned down). Yet the women come off well sometimes; it's the men who are stupid, falling into visions of false jealousy, tripped by their egos. The women are correct, but wronged. Sad universals binding East and West. Beyond that, what makes Shakespeare so at home in China is the way some characters eat bitterness, patiently don't protest, the way nothing is straight-forwardly explained, misunderstandings must be cleared by further machinations in the plot.

The Winter's Tale: The audience keeps talking; once a fight seems to break out. Shaoxing opera, performed traditionally this time, with women in all the roles. So strange to watch a tale of men's jealousy and desire performed entirely by women. Here's Hermione in a wash of fog, a favorite Chinese stage device. Hard to be a statue when the rhinestones on the headdress wires keep trembling. Finally, the jade pendant that's been hanging all night from the ceiling matches the one on Perdita's dress and she's found. A good show, worth the applause the Chinese never give, and I'm clapping, cursing the locals for not sharing this cultural habit.

The weeks of festival are done. One last time to find my bike, parked in some dark side street, ride home through the night's mix of crazy traffic and quiet, loving that mix the way the Chinese love the well-worn plots of opera, and I find the same thrill of recognition in Shakespeare: ah, the mistaken identity revealed again, ah, that good old story line. Everything just the way I like it on the stage. And on the street, I cut in front of a cycling man, ringing my bell, the clear voice of the untamed shrew.

Outside the Law

Our foreign faces grant a privilege we take advantage of, letting them slip us through the gates that otherwise would be closed, pretending we don't understand the language when someone shouts for us to wait or turn back. Dylan sang, "to live outside the law, you must be honest." To live outside the law in China, all we need is round eyes, the wrong shape nose.

Only foreigners would set off endless rounds of fireworks on the waterfront to celebrate Guy Fawkes Day, stumbling in the mud, burning our thumbs on cigarette lighters. We gather a huge crowd, coming so close we worry about their safety, try to shoo them away from the rockets. We should have worried about our own safety on another fireworks night, lighting strung-together bangs on the Jin Jiang Hotel's lawn. We learned later that some foreign dignitary was housed in the hotel, that his bodyguards might have mistaken our bangs for machine guns. The hotel's one security man didn't tell us that, only stood at the lawn's edge, watching us shinny up the flag pole to hang the little cages that erupt in singing birds when the fuse is lit, knowing he ought to stop us, knowing he couldn't, grinning and scowling at the same time.

I know I'm not supposed to climb the under-reconstruction/deconstruction steps of the closed-down Jin Jiang Club, its French architecture a reminder of the decadent grandeur of the old days. But I do anyway, trying to hide from the Japanese joint-venture carpenters, stealing past the bowling alley, the swimming pool, the ballroom with its stained glass ceiling, boarded up now. Out on the roof's wide balcony, I step between the rusty nails and junked plaster. The garden stretches below me, full of singing birds, its grass and trees the only lush green in this city. The Japanese foreman catches me on the way down, but only to say he knows me, has seen me jogging around the Jin Jiang's walks. Now I make this lawn my jogging track on crystalline winter mornings, and in the summer my beach, with only the gardeners there to stare at my bikini. I slip easily through a rent in the sagging wooden fence, beside the dead fountain, careful not to fall into its cluttered swamp.

One night the foreigners put our own tapes on the Jin Jiang sound system, dance past closing time between the tables on the bar's red carpet. Under their long gowns the waitresses sway, and the bartender under his rack of long-stemmed glasses. Just coming on duty, the night watchmen pause in the doorway, happy for something to break their shift's routine.

My friend Xue, a teacher and writer, is also talented with her needle and generously sews me clothes. One day on our way to "serious business," to shopping for silk, Xue and I make what we think will be a quick pass through an art exhibit, the latest experiments of some young men with Western abstract. But one of the painters catches me—a foreign face, a doctor of literature—so I must be important, worth giving a long explanation of every painting, with poor Xue stuck in the act of translator. I'm neither important nor rich in my country, but here Peggy and I hail the late night cabs we could never afford at home, ride miles across the sleeping city to her residence and back to my hotel, lounging in the back seat, smoking, the windows rolled down for the summer breeze.

At five a.m. all cabs are sleeping. Four of us leave the party in a friend's room and waltz the streets back, singing, to our own hotel. Our schedules intersect with those of the Chinese, rising early to noodles, setting up the market stalls. But the tall, solid metal gates of the Jin Jiang are still locked. And somehow Steve hurdles over, opening the inside latch before the startled watchmen can protest.

We know it's the arrogance of foreign transients who have nothing left to lose, breaking laws that don't exist yet, because no one has done such things before. The laws will come, because we have. In the meantime, the worst that anyone can do is send us home.

EASTER DINNER

Once I've gone back home, I know I'll wish a plate of *jiaozi*, crescent-shaped steamed dumplings, would appear at my table, with a dish of good black Zhenjiang vinegar to dip them in. Or I'll dream of that little restaurant in a hot Beijing side-street, the bowl of white *dofu*, almost translucent, floating in a cold cherry-flavored soup. Such memories will be my new nostalgia. But here in China, nostalgia takes a different shape.

I recall the farewell words of my friend Orv: "At least you know you're going to a country where you won't grow tired of the food, even after a year." Orv, like me then, had never been to China, only Chinatown. We imagined giant prawns, hot with Sichuan spice and garlic, tiny pancakes thick with strips of pork and plum sauce. We imagined the year unwinding, day after gourmet day. Months of *Dim Sum* and dumplings.

Sometimes a country's food tastes best outside that country. In China, food is seasonal, not hot-house. Tomatoes in the market, bright red and sweetly perfect for a month, then gone. White cabbage the only vegetable all winter. Regions define cooking styles—in Shanghai, everything comes drenched in rapeseed oil. The one cheese is white and rubbery, available only at the foreign food store, rumored to come from

Inner Mongolia, known to taste like a cross between Velveeta and what one might, under duress or cavalierly, name a cheese.

The foreigners begin to talk about food. At first we do it the way people anywhere will, an easy topic for strangers, introducing themselves through intimate bits of diet—a favorite wine, a pet recipe for summer fruits. Everyone learns I can't stand chicken—a disadvantage in China where the live smell of it fills the market and plucked bodies hang from the windows. We become friends; we talk about food now for the pleasure of it, as sensualists do everywhere. Two months into our year, we're hungry and nostalgic. We talk constantly of food, not wishing we were home, but wishing we had some taste of it here. We admit we want that Western decadence: variety. We torture ourselves, listening again and again to Paul describing how he smokes a fresh-caught salmon. The day a tin arrives from home, the secret is passed around to a select few. Generosity becomes important, and knowing the right friends.

Most of the foreigners are housed in hotel rooms; we eat in restaurants. But Carl and Kelly have two hotplates in their room and sometimes they borrow a tiny portable oven. Paul and I are friends with Carl and Kelly. The price of admission to their dinners is one bottle of French wine, imported to the store at my hotel. It costs a not inconsequential portion of our salaries. The dinners are worth every Chinese *fen*.

Next Sunday will be Easter, and we've discussed the dinner for days, the five courses, beginning with a pasta prepared by Carl, our resident New York Italian, with the last of the extra virgin olive oil from home. We've combed the street markets, hit the joint-venture French bread shop, ridden our bikes to the foreign food stores for wine and rum and pineapple juice to make the rum go farther. Somehow Kelly's even found bright Florida-big oranges, an extravagance to grace the rim of the rum glass.

Finally, it's Easter. It's early afternoon, and Kelly and I perch hip to hip on a luggage rack next to the bathroom sink, peeling a bowl of tiny shrimp. Paul's beside us, chopping potatoes on the bathroom counter. Carl's hungover, fixing rum drinks. The glasses tinkle like tiny church bells, with ice frozen from purified water. In the oven by the bed, the marinated lamb is roasting the room with garlic. Stacked tapes tower beside the deck, our own versions of *kyrie eleison*—Springsteen, The Police, some bootlegged Rolling Stones. The wine is lined up on the window sill, one bottle for each of us. On the table, the long opium pipe, with Chinese hash purchased on the street two blocks from this hotel.

We eat and drink for hours. Incense from the pipe drifts happily around the room. We are washed in the lamb's garlic juices. We are risen. We are not talking about food.

FINDING MY WAY

Traveler, there is no map; you make your map by walking.

Asunny day in late April. I decide to try to find the Cemetery of the Revolutionary Martyrs, to visit the grave of Rou Shi, a young writer killed by the Kuomintang in the years before Liberation, when suspected communists were lined up near the Longhua monastery, under the tall shadow of the pagoda, in front of a firing squad. The cemetery is marked on my tourist map of Shanghai, but I've learned by now that Chinese maps hold a whimsical relation to what's real. Still, I pack the map for reference and start off on my bike.

A few miles out, I pass Longhua, then ride on into unpaved streets, finally heading down some pot-holed dust in a kind of developing suburb, with several buildings underway. Nothing passes me but trucks. I ask directions from a man in a field and find I'm on the right road. Delighted, I leap on my bike and the pedals lock, throwing the chain inside the battered cover where the bolts have rusted shut. A truck gears past, wrapping me in dust. I'm stranded. No cabs will ever pass here and I can't walk the miles back with the pedals on the bike locked.

Nothing is so eloquent as a body in stunned desperation.

The man I spoke to earlier picks up his tools and joins me, prying at the cover on the bike. The metal tears at his hands; he twists and hammers till suddenly the cover's off, the chain's replaced. Knowing how the Chinese won't accept a tangible thanks, I try it anyway, offering cigarettes because I know most men here smoke, finally coaxing him to take two *yuan* in foreign exchange, a currency so treasured that even the politest sense of hospitality can't keep refusing it forever.

The dust path turns back into real road. At Caoxi Park, I stop at the ticket booth to ask about the cemetery, but I don't know the word, know only how to say "dead people" in Chinese. So I try charades, pantomime the martyrs lining up, the Kuomintang with their rifles, the martyrs falling down. The two women who sell tickets to the park are bewildered but amused. I write the name in *pinyin*, the Western alphabetic version of Chinese the country's developed to aid the foreign helpless. But the locals don't need *pinyin*, and so they're out of practice, spell any word in endless variations. Finally, I draw pictures of tombstones. Oh, inside, the women say, pleased to find this happy ending to the puzzle, and sell me a ticket to the park.

Inside, I find quiet pavilions and those large decorative rocks the Chinese find aesthetic, that always look suspiciously to me like concrete, artificially gouged and shaped. There's an old temple, boarded up, and a lovely entry gate, but no cemetery. I realize that my tombstones looked like rocks.

The road again, a big wide one this time, with four or maybe five lanes—nothing's ever definite about a Chinese traffic pattern. Across the lanes of trucks and buses, I see what seems a cemetery on my left, an arched gate opening into green and ordered space. But cycling in, I see it's not a monument to revolutionary history, it's a working graveyard for the recent dead. People with black armbands pass me, some carrying the big paper flower wreaths that get recycled for another death. I walk my bike now, out of place, asking over and over about the revolutionary martyrs, finally asking in an of-

141

fice, asking the most handsome man I've ever seen in China, a lean angular face and black thick hair above his revolutionary green. What grave do you want, he questions, what name? Rou Shi, I say, and know it's stupid. This is not the name of a brother, dead within the last ten or twenty years. So I go on— the Kuomintang, the anti-communists, the rifles. Everything but Kuomintang I say in English.

The man calls an even handsomer one, who speaks a little of my language. Older this time, with a slow, half-smiling dignity, the same green jacket. I find myself wondering what awful crime against the state these men must have committed, what bureaucratic mind assigned two men like this to clerk in graveyards. The thought is out of place, like me, the Western mind equating beauty with a singles bar.

I receive directions, gently given. Up the path, to the right of the red house, there you'll find it. But there is no red house, only a red brick building, and beside it rows of more brick rooms, open on one side, with a crowd of mourners spilling out each one, the air filled with a terrible wailing grief. The smoke from all the separate rooms pours out one tall cremation chimney. I hear a child crying Papa, the Chinese name the same as English, hear scattered voices say *ena guo ning*, the Shanghai word for foreigner, repeated not in anger but surprise.

I take the road. And there, beside the graveyard stands another gate, this time with a huge stone monument of workers and a naked woman, standing up out of their chains, ranged together in an arch. Beyond them, peace and broad walks laid out beside a mass of trees. Beyond that, a stone pinnacle with a red star and wreaths. Rectangles of bushes frame the graves, with solid tombstones, the names carved in Chinese characters and snapshots of the dead below them. The first big stone I see marks a collective grave, twelve photos of young men and women. One of them is Rou Shi. The grave is strewn with paper flowers, the ground red like blood or wine where the rain has faded tissue roses, the grass there worn away, perhaps from so many feet that have come to stand, to lay the blossoms. The black smoke from the chimney of the recent dead drifts over, but I cannot hear the screams that fell across these bodies, buried now too deep and long for sound.

I feel safer here, inside this older violence. History makes a peace that all the living share, all equally foreign to the past and death. I wander through the cemetery's hall of martyrs, full of documents, photos of their homes and faces, the scraps of life they left behind—a book, a favorite dress. They're young, well under my own nearly forty years—mostly under twenty but they look like ten or twelve. And then I find a bearded one, and read he died in 1946, the year that I was born. I think we must have passed each other. I think perhaps I've found the reason why I ride a rusting bike down dust paths that the maps don't mention, keep searching in the Shanghai heat for red stains, the faded trace of revolution's blooms.

THE BATH

Wang is a woman of many quick opinions. I don't like cheese, she tells me. I consider Italians strange. I'm sure you think my sister's more beautiful than I am. To her lover, she announces, you must be patient with me, that is your saving virtue. Her lover—a tall, angular man with a long graceful face—is laughingly patient. And one day, they'll be married.

When Wang comes to visit, she perches on the arm of whatever chair I'm sitting in, pronouncing her opinions, her eyes flashing under upswept glasses framed by straight bangs. After an hour, she asks suddenly, may I take a bath. Startled, I agree—and she produces towels, fresh underclothes, and soap from her small purse, packed like clowns inside a circus car. She disappears into the foreign luxury of a private bathroom where the tub is long and porcelain, where a flushing toilet with a seat is known as Western, so different from the trough where Chinese women squat. The shower becomes a mystery to be solved: a hand-held spigot shaped like a telephone receiver, with a winding coil—a long-distance wash. Half-dressed, Wang emerges again with another question. Don't you have hot water? Yes, but erratic, and not the fine full spray she'd expected, dreaming at home, standing up in her cold square concrete tub. The luxury of foreigners in China—

another quick opinion disappointing as the taste of cheese. Still, she makes the water, or the pleasure, last an hour in the bath.

Little Liang is also a young woman of opinions, and her English skills grow as quickly as her love of foreign ways and friends. Last week she watched approvingly while I dressed, applied the decadence of colored lines and shadow to my eyes. I've given her some of my clothes; today she tells me that she's redesigned them and "they're getting beautiful." This is not an insult but a compliment. She has published a story on the need to be graciously open with one's foreign friends.

Liang has the same stuffed tiny purse as Wang, the same faith in my answer when she asks to use the bath. The first time, she bathes so long that I grow bored. I go out for beer; the door's still closed when I return. I begin to worry; people have been known to drown. I knock and she appears, dressed now, a blush of lipstick, her short black cap of hair freshly shining. I like your bath, she says, and comes back often. Sometimes she lies down in the tub and holds the showerhead above her, the spray like warm rain. Other days she fills the tub and says it's just like swimming. Only better. At the beach, the ocean is too vast and she's afraid.

Liang dislikes my Chinese lover. Wang has never met him. No one Chinese knows he is my lover. Some things are simply not done in this country and little is safely talked of.

My lover is as young and angular as Wang's future husband, more graceful, and less patient. He never asks to use my bathtub, but one day he suggests that I might like to bathe. A strange request because, of course, the tub is mine, always there to be filled when I wish, and can't he see how freshly I've come from it. But I say none of this, say simply no, and consider the issue closed. Because our mutual language skills are minimal, it is not often useful to probe beneath the surface of his questions.

Later, I go into the bath to wash some glasses at the sink.

He follows, opening his arms. At last I understand. The bathroom puts a second and more private door between him and the Chinese maid, who sometimes enters unexpectedly to bring fresh thermoses of water, dust around the mat, and watch who visits.

My lover wants to form his own opinions of things foreign, but not quickly. Like my other Chinese friends, he teaches me that pleasure means a long time in the bath.

THE WIZARD

The Dalai Lhama is the Wizard of Oz. Only you don't dance down yellow brick roads to find him, arms around a straw man and a tin one, the wind blowing your braids over the rainbow. You circle the Jokhung Temple from before dawn till long past sunset. You stretch full length on the ground, get up and step to where your hands last touched, and bow again, sliding face down into the dust. You climb the thousands of tall stone steps to the richly furnished chambers in the Potala Palace, empty now because the Lhama's fled the Chinese, who've come to tolerate the Tantric opium of Tibet's fanaticist Buddhism, but not its wedding of religious leadership with temporal powers.

In the temples, there are statues of the Lhamas, doll-like with round pink faces. In place of the absent one, on the altars sits his tall triangular peaked yellow cap with long earflaps, the sort of thing you'd wear in Oz. Everyone wants photos of the Lhama now in exile; monks and pilgrims come up with their hands out, their one major phrase in English: " Dalai Lhama photo? Dalai Lhama photo?" Any one will do, even a cheap Xerox from some story in *Time* or *Newsweek*. Wily, well-informed tourists come with stacks of them, often. for barter or a way to bribe the monks into letting them take the otherwise forbidden photos in the temples. We're less

prepared and have to endlessly repeat the answer *mei you*—
"not have." Eventually we learn the same phrase in Tibetan—
min dun. Once, at Drepung Monastery, some boy monks devise a new mantra, and follow us through the temple, laughing, chanting *mei you, min dun, mei you, min dun, mei you, mei
you, min dun*. At Ganden, some monks invite us, already dizzy
with the altitude, to climb more stairs and ladders to their
quarters, where we force a few polite sips of the rancid yak
butter tea. The monks thumb through Carl's Tibetan guide
book, pleased at finding their own monastery pictured there—
the buildings destroyed in the Chinese war and sanded quickly
to ancient ruins by Tibetan winds, now being restored. Below us on a roof, a boy plays a long plaintive horn, above the
yaps of twenty mangy curs. The monks discover a photo of
the Dalai Lhama in Carl's book. *"You, you,"* they shout teas-
ingly, "have," "have." See, you really did possess one after
all.

Outside on the Ganden hills we eat lunch, share the last of
our sardines with a beggar, one of many in Tibet. Does he
think that the Lhama's return would ease his poverty? It's an
ascetic religion; perhaps an empty belly doesn't matter. Maybe
believing in the absent Lhama is enough, like that rumored
Wizard in his palace. The strength and the fanaticism of the
belief are the same. I've read that monks—at least in earlier
days—ate pills made from Dalai Lhama shit. The sixth ruler
led a double life; he was a lover of wine and a womanizer as
well as being the Dalai Lhama. Perhaps where something so
simply human as shit was sacred, these behaviors did not
constitute a fall from grace. Perhaps his gold and jeweled
chorten—a burial cairn like a cross between a giant helmet
and a bridal bonnet—sits with the others in the high dark
chamber in the Potala, an atmosphere of strange peace and
audible quiet in the room, one cloth prayer wheel turning in
the heat from a yak butter lamp.

This is a religion of compassion. The monk, taking up the
paper upon which is written the effigy of a spying ghost, must

break the ghost's bones with compassion for both the ghost and its victims. This is a religion of a myriad rituals. No wonder the best minds among the men often became monks— how else devise such intricate prayers and steps, how else remember them? A religion of exotic devices, where the best trumpets are said to be made from the thigh bone of a Brahmin girl. A religion of patience where monks may chant endlessly to ward off hostile forces or to become one with a god, where a monk may spend days tapping colored grains of sand into a perfect mandala that is swept into a vase at the festival's end and poured into a stream.

Somehow such devotion leaves me fascinated and depressed. This country with its stark brown peaks and brilliant sky, its plains lying high above the mountains of most places, this country is a dream beyond the ken of Oz. And yet the energy of so many is sucked into days of repetitive prostrations, the fierce attachment to the photos of a round-faced man in glasses, to an empty yellow hat. Maybe the smiling boy monks would be better off without their wizard. But what would occupy their time then in these isolated heights?

There is a saying that if you are pure in heart, everyone is a buddha; if your heart is impure, everyone is ordinary. Not a bad set of choices. The sort of thing a kindly wizard might ascribe to and urge his followers to do the same. Either way it seems you win.

AND I ALWAYS MEANT
TO TURN FORTY IN PARIS

The airport bus pulls out of Lhasa, past the river, the bridge so heavily festooned with prayer flags it seems woven from them, more like a ragged red, blue, and yellow hammock than a footbridge. Prayer flags wave on spindly branches at each corner of the low stone and clay homes. The road follows the flat bed of the river, fingers of water always threatening to spill over. The river is a long, milky blue fish with splashes of slate fins. The brown barren mountains stretch away on either side.

On the bus, the young Tibetan men drink beer from cups; their women laugh. People and luggage crowd the aisles. It's more than an hour's drive to the airport. The bus stops once, seemingly for no reason. Then the men climb out the windows, walk two steps from the bus, and piss.

A few miles from the airport sits a concrete hotel. We're checked in for the night. The plane to Chengdu is the only flight out, leaving only once each morning. Though it's summer, the evening air turns cold; inside, the hotel's a bleaker prefab chill. Not much to order in the restaurant that opens haphazardly for an hour. No soda, no tea, not even hot water. Only the beer I won't drink at this altitude. I settle for a gritty bowl of rice, try not to watch the man beside me swatting flies with his chopsticks, using the same pair to eat.

People wander the parking lot. I sit, watch lightning in the mountains. Then a brown wave like smoke moves quickly toward us, obscuring every ridge it passes. The wave is dust, carried on the high hard wind that hits us now, ripping the small trees. Nothing to do but press our faces to the windows, listening to the glass moan, or wait in our rooms till the Chinese shut the lights and water down at ten.

Mostly, foreigners are roomed with foreign and pay more. As a teacher, I pay Chinese prices. The clerk has seen my red work card, and roomed me with a Chinese woman and her tiny mother, thinking I can speak Chinese. We try a bit of conversation, amiably accepting my lack of skill, which seems just another inevitability, like the toilet that won't flush correctly or the knowledge that the lights are centrally controlled and will blaze again before dawn, when the Chinese attendants will bang on our door.

In the morning we rush to dress, then wait forever for the bus. Wait again at the tiny airport with no plane in sight and finally a message of delay chalked on the wall. We're shunted from one room to another one with long benches. But at least there's tea, and I have cough drops I can suck for their sugar when the hunger really hits. It's July 14, Bastille Day and my fortieth birthday. I always meant to turn this age in Paris. I think the French know how to celebrate a revolution better than the Chinese. More glamor, more extremes of passion, more long-stemmed crystals of good wine. I think about the free drinks all those Frenchmen might have bought me. I turn to the group of Scandinavian travelers beside me. One more China delay, I sigh, not the best beginning for my birthday.

The Chinese have a sixth sense for delays. They don't sit, tensely waiting. They lounge, then before anything's announced, suddenly scoop up their bags and rush to head the line. I take my movement cues from them and still end up last, milling onto the small plane, finding a window to watch the long landscape of cloud and jagged peaks slip into the humid green of summer Chengdu.

151

Civilization's what you name it. After the ascetic heights of Lhasa, the fanatic pilgrims, and the intricate mandalas of the temple walls, I name this city easier civilization. I make brass and marble hotel lobbies part of my definition, and the air conditioning, the freedom to drink beer again inside this sea-level heat, the steam of a shower in the common bath at the end of a carpeted hall.

I plan my birthday. Kelly, who was on her way from Lhasa to Nepal with too much luggage, has given me a dress. I go out to buy high heels to match it. Shoes cost so little in China that I can afford such extravagance. If they don't fit well, later I can throw them away. I know I've returned to civilization when I find a shop selling lipstick and sticky cheap nail polish. The young shopgirl's more than civilized, her own face laughing and lightly painted, approving my choice of colors. Back at the hotel, I smear the polish on my freshly showered toes.

In the cavernous dining hall, I sit at the far end, surveying, eating eggplant that's Sichuan hot with chiles. The Scandinavians come in and join me. One of them, a long, handsome blonde man, whose name I can't recall, whose address I will eternally regret I was too shy to ask, sells shoes. He imports Italian ones to Holland, to Amsterdam where twenty years ago I first got truly stoned on marijuana, given me by a blonde man with eyes as clear and blue as Christ's in Renaissance paintings. I remember I was too shy then to travel with him to Edinburgh, and took my scheduled plane home to my lover in Chicago, who left me not long after. I remember I meant to turn forty in Paris, not Lhasa or Chengdu. I remember choices are what you make them.

After dinner we go up to the roof of the Chengdu Hotel, sit outside around metal tables with umbrellas. One Scandinavian woman and I want wine, but the waiter tells us we can buy it only by the bottle and the cheapest one costs thirty *kuai*, far beyond my teacher's salary. We settle for the local beer. The man from Amsterdam appraises my birthday shoes.

The Chengdu air hangs thick around us, humid as fog. We're unreal in this rooftop bar that could float somewhere in Chicago, the city lost below us and the rich green fields beyond it, the clumps of trees leaning into the white stone farm homes, where men with shaved heads, baggy shorts, and long white shirts recline in tall bamboo chairs. The heat makes Sichuan a gracious province, lush and slow.

The man from Amsterdam and his friend have gone inside to the bar. They emerge now, with long-stemmed crystal between their fingers and a bottle of white wine. A city's what you name it. Anyplace your life turns forty, things can happen. Cheap shoes turn into Cinderella's, and a French accent becomes a Dutch.

VI

Modern Flights

LOVING BOEING

I've always hated the Boeing Company—the military industrial complex, the cruise missile, the freeway traffic jams when the shift lets out, the way everyone who works there says the name wrong, calls it Boeings. But I swear when I get home to Seattle, I'll kneel down, like the Pope arriving in some South American country he wants to impress, and kiss the Boeing parking lot's soil. Why? Because the planes in China function more by luck and whimsy than by science, and boarding, every time I saw the brand name and recognized the old-style cabins of my youth, I felt a little safer. I could tell myself this plane rolled off the line and passed inspection once, no matter what it's been through in these twenty Chinese years.

There are no air fare wars in China. Only one airline, the state-owned CAAC. But there are different prices—for the Chinese, for the foreigners, for the twilight zone of Hong Kong residents and the foreigners whose work cards make them honorary Chinese. And there are back door dealings with the agent, who tells you every seat's sold out, but extra *kuai* and bottles of his favorite wine can magically buy tickets. Not even back door dealings can produce a round-trip; there are no computers, phones are unreliable, no way to know how many seats are open at the other end. The day you get somewhere you stand in line to buy a ticket back.

This may prove fruitless. In Kunming we stood before the counter labeled Shanghai, waiting for an agent. Waiting a long time till a woman said that agent's ill, no tickets can be sold today to Shanghai.

Even ticketed, you might not fly. And even with the sun shining here and at your destination, delays or cancellations get blamed on weather. Yet I boarded a plane to Beijing once in a sudden snow. Climbed on beside the serious men in green fur-collared army greatcoats, and the atmosphere seemed right, seemed like an earlier decade, an earlier war, the austerity of heading north in the hard mid-winter cold.

It wasn't weather that kept me waiting for twelve hours for my flight home. At first, some Chinese mystery and the ever-optimistic way they shift departure times, acknowledging the delay little by little in hopeful segments. The truth circulated in rumors, some mechanism burned out in the plane's radio, and, of course, no parts available in Shanghai. The rumors spread through hours of sitting, with the only restaurant shut down, the Chinese passing out the plane's snack, and the endless arguments. Someone was being flown to Beijing for the parts or perhaps they'd come in on the next flight. At last, a Beijing plane arrived that matched the Boeing jet we meant to navigate the ocean in. A quick substitution of parts, and the exit doors were flashing. Time to board.

And time to eat, from the cardboard box that holds the same food every flight, breakfast, lunch, or dinner: candy, sweet breads, pastry dripping with artificial cream. Time for the presents the airline always passes out: a bag of cookies or maybe a gaudy, fake-jeweled pin, sometimes a model of the Boeing. On one trip, in late January, the flight attendants handed passengers leftover Christmas cards, the kind with computer-generated music when you open them. The plane's cabin filled with "Jingle Bells."

Cheap thrills substitute for service, the way gifts take the place of real food. Every pilot's military trained and makes jet-fighter landings, coming in too fast, especially for the short runways. Landing is a surge and a sudden fish-tail brake, a dance from wheel to wheel.

Once, in the middle of the Pacific, a crackling, burning sound began above our heads. Everyone called the flight attendants and the engineer—who looked up idly and disappeared. One attendant was more forthcoming than the others. Well, she said, the engines are still running, no reason to be upset. I kept staring at the label: Boeing 747. I felt my knees begin to genuflect.

PASSPORT EYES

C ertain young men and women have them. They look straight at the foreigner they're talking with, smiling, the women with a teasing cast to their lashes, the men copying the intensity of heroes in the movies. You seem to be the center of their gaze, but if you look much closer into their eyes, you'll find a vision of escape, a dream of foreign places, just a marriage license and passport away. Such love is wisely blind, focused clearly on a purpose, and the defects of potential mates can be ignored, as long as the lover's foreign and planning to return home.

Some school days at lunch time, we gather in the office shared by Suzanne and Paul. Richard comes over from the law school, and Paul makes real coffee in the filter pot, Suzanne brewing her own weak cup from the leftover grounds. Other friends and students drop in, and lately a young woman from a nearby school, who lounges laughing in a big chair, with an ease more foreign than local. That woman, say Paul and Richard, doesn't just have passport eyes; she wears passport goggles.

One day, Richard brings a letter from some young man he's run into at an airport; they've chatted while waiting for a plane. It seems the young man has a cousin who likes all things foreign. He encloses a photo. "If you're not going for her," he writes, "then you can maybe find a job for me in the United States."

A friend tells me that a man she knows questioned another at our school about the teachers. Don't you have some foreign women there, he asked. Yes, replied the other, but one's old and the other's ugly. Three foreign women teach at our school, but one is sixty-eight, beyond even the reach of passport eyes. According to the story, I'm old and Suzanne is ugly. Neither of us is pleased.

Still, we forgive them, understanding how desperately they want to leave, how circumscribed their lives can be in China, how little they know of the problems they'll encounter somewhere else. We know wearing passport eyes takes courage in a country where morals strictly govern even local liaisons and spending unofficial time with foreigners can be dangerous.

Sometimes the foreign women feel generous, feel we should hold our left hands aloft for a ring, like the Statue of Liberty with her torch. In a book, I find an old picture of Judy Garland, Lana Turner, and Hedy Lamarr. The caption notes they numbered seventeen husbands among them. We could do our part for freedom, I say to Peggy, a variation on Hollywood stars. We could marry them, one after the other, divorce them safely off the boat in Reno, planting their feet on truly U.S. soil.

Sometimes the truth is not so humorous. Sometimes love gets in the way of passport plans, and marriage becomes real enough to say no, in both languages. The day before my plane lifts out of Shanghai, my Chinese lover closes my door behind him, and when I open it to say goodby once more, he doesn't turn, walking slowly down the hall. I cannot see his eyes.

CLIMBING MT. HUANGSHAN

S aturday afternoon TV, a documentary of Huangshan,
of some Chinese painter in his eighties who climbs it
every year to paint the clouds and mist curling around
its peaks, nothing that delicate and jagged anywhere but in
China, unfolding in the centuries of silk scrolls.

Carl climbed it. Suzanne and Antoinette did too, last year.
I refuse. In the States, I live near mountains, hate driving them
in winter, and love the other seasons when I park the car, my
boots finding their way up tiny paths of cedar needles, un-
even with rocks and long gnarled roots. Nobody else going
up or down, the songs of invisible birds in moss-shawled trees.

That's why I won't climb Huangshan, with its stairs carved
in rock, the path jammed like an escalator at a Christmas shopping mall. Eighty-thousand visitors in two days, says the *China
Daily*. Several thousand stranded on the steep slopes in a sudden downpour, and one woman accidently pushed off a cliff,
one of the hundred injured or dead in a year, falling when
somebody elbowed ahead to the top.

Still, the crowds keep climbing. And my Chinese friends
ask aren't I lonely in my hotel room—one bedroom and a
bath and a large closet too, all to myself. More people died
on the Long March than on Huangshan—not just on the mountain range they straggled through, barefoot in the snow, but

in the grasslands where the open green stretched endlessly without a face, except their own. We're Chinese, the survivors said, we couldn't bear the landscape without people.

Like them, I step so many days without familiar referents here, no footing I can trust. At the school, Paul's lecture on Canada turns me homesick. The slide of the man frying fish at his morning camp. I can feel the plaid wool and the denim, the fresh-from-the-sleeping-bag scruffiness, the cool damp. And feel ungrounded, no homely routine, nothing to test my judgments against—this novel that I read could be brilliant or silly, I could wear a Chinese red bride's suit and marry this man, live happily or not. Just in time a friend reminds me that we'd live in one room, with a grandmother, pulls me from the cliff.

I'd get happily elbowed off by love, but this is only vertigo, a foreigner adrift in crowds, unable to name what's real. Then Martin sends me photos that he took in China, scenes I live so frequently I forget to notice, to pick out like the camera's eye the one old woman in a stream of them crossing the street.

No peaks are as delicate, and as crowded as Huangshan's. I'll leave them to the eighty-thousand climbers, to old painters setting up their easels. I'll wait to set my foot on rocks as singular and solid as real love. To be the one old woman captured in a crowd.

THE ANCIENT KEEPS COLLIDING WITH
THE TACKY MODERN

"You're leaving for a year in China!" my friend Michael exclaimed, envy seeping over the long distance line between Albuquerque and Seattle. "I wonder if they keep a copy of the *I Ching* in every hotel room, like the *Gideon Bible.*"

No *I Ching* here, Michael, and no little red book of Mao. The first discredited by the anti-traditional bias that marked movements like the Cultural Revolution, the second by the madness of the Cultural Revolution itself. Both have the status of museum pieces now, not the daily substance of hotel drawers. And thankfully, the Western missionaries' hold was never strong enough to leave behind that many bibles.

I brought with me the typical foreigner's vision of China: jagged peaks inked on scrolls, the glitter of the Forbidden City, the "teeming millions" in the streets and rice fields, the Long March, the *I Ching* and the Tao, the poems of Li Po, the banners streaming around big portraits of Mao. Disparate pieces, scattered like the dots on a page in a child's coloring book. I'd never bothered to try to connect them and find what picture they revealed, maybe understanding, even in my foreign ignorance, that this couldn't be done. I also brought a less typical approval of the aims of Liberation, an honest appreciation for red.

I come from an infant country, compared to China, compared to almost every other nation. Like any toddler, it thinks
itself the center of the universe, and tries to bully everybody
else into waiting on its whims. "The United States," I reply,
when people ask about my origins. "A hard country to be
from." I try to disassociate myself from the toddler's behavior.

Perhaps that's why I hate to see the Western touches spreading here, suspecting, like some conservative on the Central
Committee, that sleek cars bring a love of capitalism, that re-
placing bamboo with plastic leads to thoughts as fake and
superficial as the gloss, that the latest Rambo movie packing
the Chinese theatres supports an imperialist macho, that soon
I won't be able to walk these late night streets safely alone.

Nobody has a sieve to strain the good influences and stop
the bad. Nobody would agree on good and bad. Traveling
south, Suzanne and I laugh when we find a tiny restaurant
named McDonald's of Guilin, and of course we pose for photos beside the sign. But we're happy to find the food's still
slow and Chinese. In Xi'an Peggy and I stop, amazed to hear
disco blaring from what seems a punk shop, with imitation
"new wave" clothes and jewelry, sexy underwear hanging in
the street beside the door. We find this more important cul-
turally than the museum. We think the proprietor should give
us a discount in return for our obvious show of interest in
the merchandise, a testimonial that these items reflect foreign
taste. We don't call these things dangerous like Rambo. Not
everyone would agree.

My Chinese friends consider the goods I want to buy old
fashioned. "Sibyl wants to dress like a grandmother," they
laugh, when I express an interest in the old women's baggy
mid-calf pants, their grey shirts buttoned in a slant to the high
collars. What attracts me most is not the antique, the elegantly
ornate, but the simple grace of grandma fashions, the lines of
tiny bamboo chairs—things not for sale anywhere. The Chinese love bright plastic, the tacky versions of Western styles

in local shops. The foreigners are supposed to love the jade and carpets that pack the special multi-storied "Friendship Stores."

I wander the old section of Shanghai, down narrow street markets stacked with balloons in bags, Woolworth jewelry, garish synthetic sweaters. And turn the corner into Yu Garden, with its sixteenth-century pagodas, heavy rosewood chairs, carp in the ponds below the delicate bridges, hours of detailed carving everywhere. Better, but the alleys beyond seem better yet, the low white crumbling homes with slate-tiled roofs joined together in a rambling line, a visual rhythm of shutters and blue rag mops hung up beside pots and baskets. Cement sinks outside the homes, tables for chopping the night's greens and chicken, an assembly line of hands mashing pork into balls, wrapping dough around them.

People seem to lose their sense of aesthetics when they become Westernized. I know this is the arrogant opinion of one who has a choice of options, who's come full circle to despise the modern. I understand the inconvenience of those outdoor sinks. I know the people mill outside because their rooms are dank and crowded, too hot in summer, too cold in winter, and the baby's cries echo too loudly in narrow stone walls. But they're also in the street because they like its energy, take an interest in what passes, feel lonely without the contact.

I hate the concrete blocks of apartments going up, demolishing these streets, though I know they must hold more rooms, and larger ones, with indoor sinks and maybe even private toilets. Each apartment has a balcony, and the concrete sea resolves itself to individual efforts at beauty, each balcony filled with potted plants, softening the grey.

I'm just a romantic, an anachronism like the last man who washed money in a San Francisco hotel, a holdover from the days when ladies wore white gloves and liked to keep them unsoiled. (He died this year, and the tradition with him.) I like to travel outside the Westernness of cities, to small market towns around Kunming, where the minorities (the non-Han Chinese) keep traditions, carving the shaved pig on a table for the New Year, pouring into towns in carts pulled by bony, spirited ponies, with bells on the harness, red ribbons in their manes, the whole family standing up in the cart behind, the women wearing colored scarves and headdresses. I like this passage into another century, with centuries behind it, even knowing how this life is hard, the laundry scrubbed on rocks in a brown stream, the bodies muddy from digging in clay fields.

Outside Yangshuo, on the Li River whose misty peaks are featured in so many silk scrolls, I watch the barefoot men pole thin rafts, one cormorant on the front, tied with a line around its throat so the bird will fish but not swallow the big ones, bring them back to the raft for dinner. In Louyang, I lean over the bridge, see a man in waders, studying the water. He makes a Zen toss of his black, silken net. It swirls like a flamenco dancer's skirt, then cuts through the water, leaving a pattern. Immediately, he pulls it back, easily as drawing in a wet silk hem. On the rocks, he picks out twenty fish, drops them over his shoulder into a woven basket on his back, where they leap silver. I'd rather watch these men than trawlers or the harpoon cannon of a whaling ship.

Call this a stubborn refusal to admit the superiority of convenience. Call it romantic affectation. Like Maurice Chevalier, who could speak a perfectly native English and trained himself to speak it with a French accent to please his foreign audience. Inconvenient, but appealing.

China's an ancient mix of contradictions, incongruous habits. At the theatre, between the dance of the sleeves, with the long folds of silk swirling, and the dance of the men in grey, moving with the dignity of the unearthed terra cotta warriors that guard the emperor's 300 BC tomb, there's bound to be a dance of the hula hoops, spinning garishly around slim waists, lit by the high tech of a black light. I'm contradictory and incongruous too. I'm glad to see a ghettoblaster sitting above the painted chest and flowered quilts in an Inner Mongolian yurt. I'm gladder still to see the plastic roses and the bottle of cleaning fluid left leaning casually against them on the altar before the Buddha. I think it means that people don't take things more seriously, more sacredly than necessary.

Michael, I don't need a copy of the *I Ching* in my hotel drawer, don't want it any more than I want a bible or the five cockroaches that really live there. I guess I can go on without romance, without Karl Marx, even without my own romantic Marxism. Save your envy on the Albuquerque phone line for the wisdom that I've learned from watching men in the high grasslands of Inner Mongolia. They move the stones around on roads, to keep the drivers steering their wheels in new directions, preventing ruts. The modern West is just another stone the country has to keep on shifting.

THE BIRD FLIES

I'm really leaving. I've given my hot plate, my one kettle, and random dishes to Chinese friends who joke and say they don't just profit educationally from a foreign teacher. The rest of what won't fit in my luggage lies on the bed, abandoned to my *fus*. Jiang, a young teacher from my school, arrives to help me carry bags. At the last minute, my friend Xue calls. I've tried to reach her for a week; it turns out she's been ill, and staying at her mother's room. Now she rushes over with her husband; we madly load the cab. In the hustle, I pass my favorite *fu*, coming out the door with her bowl of noodles. Goodby, I call, *zaijian, zai a wei*. And the airport ride I thought would be nostalgic reverie flies by, full of talk.

The background sense of dread remains, the habit I've acquired here of thinking ahead to anticipate the next thing that could go wrong, the rule that could suddenly change, the rule I've never heard of before, the rule concocted on the spot. That nagging worry won't leave me till I've cleared the San Francisco customs, smiling my way past their uniforms, keeping them off my trail.

I clear Shanghai customs even faster. Xue's husband has some back-door connection, some former student who lets us all pass the first barrier dividing passengers from friends.

169

The customs officer simply notes my red work card—oh, a teacher, well, goodby—and waves me on.

We don't know that the flight will be delayed twelve hours, that I'll sit here, knowing it's useless to battle with the erratic phones to call my friends back—no way for them to enter the final departure area, too complicated for me to try to exit. At this bustling moment, we think the plane will leave on time. Xue turns toward me. "You are a bird," she says, "free to fly, but I myself am caged." There is nothing to say in the face of such truth. I step over the line of the last ticket check. I look back once, lifting my wing in farewell, the only gesture I can make now, from the other side.

AND ALL MY LIFE

I t wasn't that I wanted to go home, only that I wanted to leave China, had toyed with staying, but knew I needed some relief, some change. The tears that come as the plane drops over the sunny afternoon of San Francisco Bay are homesick only for the sudden rush of colors after a year of concrete grey.

I open the door past airport customs, find my California friend Samantha with her camera, shouting for me to stop, documenting my arrival as she did my leaving, her waiting car packed with diet soda, Doritos, and beer. The freeway seems like a sales lot filled with new cars. I can't imagine driving, getting behind my own wheel, braving the on-ramp, miles in the fast lane.

No culture shock when I hit Shanghai. Nothing there was supposed to seem familiar. The shock of coming back reverberates in tremors for a long time.

Wandering San Francisco, I suddenly find myself at the gate to Chinatown, drawn there by some instinct for home, like a Chinese fresh off the boat. But the place is too clean, no cabbages spread for sale beside the gutters, no old women selling shallots, stem by stem. It's really Hong Kong, business-minded, everyone thinking in dollars, in English and

Cantonese, not responding to my Mandarin tones, not impressed when I say I just returned from China.

I laugh at the almost empty buses, the patient waiting lines. When bureaucratic agencies, like the bank or Ma Bell, give me trouble, I say they're competing for the China Award. Waiters startle me, arriving so soon after I've sat down, ready to name the evening's specials, to light my cigarette. I watch twenty movies in a month, beginning with *A Great Wall*, where only the scenes shot in California seem foreign. For weeks, I panic when friends gather and I see the evening's stock of food or cigarettes or beer begin to run low; then I remember, it's the U.S., a 7-11 on every block.

I've only half-returned. I'm overly frightened by panhandlers, tough kids hanging out on corners, my street-wise habits rusty after the safety of China. But after months of uniformity, I'm pleased by the mix of orange Mohawks beside elderly rouged women, wearing their furs to the theatre in the August sun. I spent a whole day once in Shanghai, lingering over the ads in an old copy of *The Village Voice*, like some *National Geographic* documenting the delightfully outrageous customs of a tribe, the bewildering choice of pleasures. I remember I'm not here on a tourist visa, that my passport names this tribe as mine. Still, when I see Chinese, I say, half-jokingly but with affection, "my people." Say it without the irony we foreigners used in China, when a group of locals spit their fish bones on the table. Yet we felt closer to the Chinese than to the tourists; watching a cornfed group from Iowa, we'd say "not my people." Longtime foreigners become their own nomadic tribe. Now dinner conversations in the States seem monotonously strange: only one language in one accent, one country stamped on every passport.

China disappears into nostalgia fed by letters: a former student asks me to define love, a teacher just retiring from my school sends his regards to my "aged mother" who hasn't yet reached sixty-five. Antoinette, back in Beijing, assures me nothing's changed, describes in detail the boots she's just bought, stitched with stylish patterns, and a label with the English words "hand wash, don't dry clean" sewed firmly on the outside, part of the design. Perhaps the Chinese characters across the chests of fashionable sweatshirts in the U.S. state something equally domestic.

The newspaper clippings I receive confirm Antoinette's assessment: two peasants invent a singing candle; a Chinese guard rips a Phil Silvers t-shirt off a tourist in Tibet, confusing Silvers' bald head with the Dalai Lama's; an "electric man" in Xinjiang knocks his wife down with a charge when he touches her hair; a young Chinese poet who "organized a commune" of single people in Shanghai and "advocated free love" is sentenced to five years in prison on the charge of "hooliganism." The country's half-baked inventiveness and sense of the fantastic, its crazy extremes of embracing and resisting change continue.

My friends wait a year before they confess how terrible they thought I looked when I came home: exhausted, strung out. I don't remember looking that bad, even with my last Chinese haircut growing out in straggling layers. I remember crying often. Cried at an art gallery, surrounded by a crowd in high chic, sipping their wine and lionizing. The paintings were the latest punk distortions of a slick, throw-away society, meant to be sophisticated humor, clear to me as sheer violence—my blinders off. A high school choir at Christmas sent me back to foreigners caroling at the U.S. Consulate, the tears coming for the way our fingers grip familiarity like the edge of a cliff, and for these half-formed high school faces, the land mines of conventional futures that so many would trip into, happily or not, no way I could predict which ones would escape, no clear definition of escape.

I carry a sharpened sense of what seems just the silly excess of a spoiled country, missing the simplicity of China, wishing more of it lived here. Drawn by the music of the gongs and *erhu* strings, I drift one afternoon into a room in Chinatown, to listen with the old men and women. I note what changes happened during my year away—the gourmet deli sections even in the local supermarkets, the greater number of homeless on the street. A rich country, that could care gently for its own tribe and those of the world, and so often doesn't, injures them instead. I love its color and variety; I love the freedom that its passport gives me to escape. And all my life I'll keep on leaving, my way to grip the sharp cliff of perspective, to keep my heart from stumbling on a land mine.

KEEPSAKES

Walking down busy, narrow Sichuan Lu one afternoon, keeping well off the center of the street, I looked up to see a man peddling a bike cart loaded with junk and old doors stacked crookedly, jutting off the cart in every direction. The man shouted *"wei, wei, wei,"* just as the first sharp-edged door slammed into me. Luckily, I was walking with my arms crossed, so it was my wrist, and not my ribs, that spit blood, swelling into a sudden painful bulb, the patchwork of bruises spreading fast. The inevitable crowd gathered. The man actually laughed, behaving as if the accident were my fault. To the crowd's delight, I scolded him in Chinese, shouting over and over "You can't even say you're sorry" until he did.

The wound, of course, healed, leaving at first a small indentation where my arm curves into my wrist, later just a short white scar line, resting in a patch of skin that's pink or vaguely purple, depending on the weather.

One day when I've been home in the States a few months, I notice a good-sized bump as hard as bone has sprouted on the back of my hand, a little above the scarred wrist. I ask my doctor, and he talks about cartilage and joints leaking something that gels—a medical wisdom whose details I immediately forget. I prefer his second explanation: "It's a bible bump.

175

In the old days, people smashed them with the bible, the heaviest book in the house." I think the trauma of my wrist's collision with the Chinese door must be connected to the bump's appearance, but my doctor disagrees. I know he's wrong. If my *Qi Gong* teacher were here, he'd say the energy displaced from my wrist would have to erupt somewhere.

The folk cure intrigues me. Some days I'm tempted to try my giant annotated bible, or better yet, the complete works of Shakespeare or the *OED*. I wonder if I should shout *"wei, wei, wei"* as I slam, or if the bump itself will shout that as the energy breaks up, small bits of Chinese tones reverberating through my body. I never try it. I grow fond of the bump, the good witch silhouette it lends my left hand. And fond of the scar below it, the mark I wear as proudly as I'd carry the slash of a knife fight I'd survived—or the red kiss of a love bite.

VII

Parables of the Middle Kingdom

COUNTING THE LIONS

If I can name a thing, I understand it. I carry words like summer fireflies in my hands, a swarm of tiny torches to light the spaces I travel through. For weeks I try to name the trees that line the Shanghai streets, with their patchy tan and ivory trunks, the branches spreading from each side till they interlace above the center of the street, making a green canopy against the summer sun. Everyone gives me different names: acacia, cypress, plane. Many simply call them French trees, because the French were the first to plant them here. Finally, a friend says sycamore, and I believe him because he grew up in Ohio.

Naming the truth of anything about China is like that, something tracked and guessed at till it feels correct, and tomorrow slips away as easily as fireflies from a hand. A long-time visitor here says that after a week, he felt he could write a book about China; after six weeks, he knew he could write nothing with any sense of certainty. This is not a matter of translation, of a country with such a crazy-quilt of spoken languages that only the written word holds dialogue together, Chinese from different regions drawing characters across their palms to talk. In the Great Hall of the People, under the huge red star on the ceiling, each seat has its own translation box, with knobs to dial the speech in the delegate's language.

Somehow the language system works. I receive what's said, but the meaning of that breaks down or becomes an endless round of futile questions, like that Abbott and Costello routine where the baseball players' names are "What" and "I Don't Know" and "Who," so when you ask which player's on third, you get a helpful "I Don't Know." The truth, but not an answer.

I finish an old Chinese novel on the train and look up from its pages to watch the modern crowd around me. I can't read their faces, what they actually think and feel—their motivations as distant and unclear as those of the characters in the book. Do they really have all the melodramatic emotions of their literature, all the meditations on philosophy and principle? I know they match the tales of scheming, of rumors and saving face. And so the rest must also be true.

This is not the stereotype of inscrutability. As my friend Paul says, nothing here's inscrutable, everything is present, open, for anyone to read. My problem lies in reading. I walk into a tiny corner shop, where typically the samples of the clothes for sale are strung up randomly on hangers. I reach up for a t-shirt and find it's wet, a bit of the family's laundry hung between the merchandise. All there, displayed, but still inscrutable distinctions.

One day I realize that the poems I've written here rarely feature individual Chinese. I wonder what this says about the culture. I wonder what it says about me. Later, I'll carefully hide the identities of Chinese friends, afraid that what I write will cause them trouble, if only because it proves they've spent some private time too close to foreigners. I think perhaps I'm learning why distinctions are so hard to fathom in a place where often it seems safer to match the crowd.

I grow wiser than some foreigners, wiser than Henry Kissinger on an English TV show about China, documenting his impression of Mao as a man of mysterious power. We didn't know, says Kissinger, when we could see him and then suddenly a man arrived and said come now. Kissinger dealt only in a world of powers, not the ordinary Chinese life of schools where no one knows just when the term will end and shops that might be stocked or might have empty shelves. He thought that mystery and surprise were attributes of famous leaders. I know they are the soil of China.

And contradiction is the country's heart. Some foreign diplomat gets chauffeured in a limousine, with a procession of twenty empty cabs behind, so everywhere else in the city, there's not a cab to hail. What a fuss to make a good front, a production, but only the middle of the floor gets swept. A sleeveless blouse creates a scandal and yet the silk's so thin on every dress you look right through the patterns to the lingerie and nobody's shocked at that. Everyone's in love with the efficiency of Western high tech; the taxi driver leaves the plastic covers on the plush seats, treasures the automatic door-locks and the high-speed cornering—and still has to write ten minutes of forms for every fare. The restaurant opens in the new skyscraper, with the waitresses in some Chinese version of the Holiday Inn, green uniforms with aprons and anklets. But the carpet's coming up in balls of wool, the bar has a long running gouge, and the place has been open only a week. Every clerk is napping in the shop and still the five-year plan's complete. Every move of the opera's been perfected for centuries and still the lighting's corny.

The truth lies in the contradictions, and humor in accepting them. My own heart beats these pendulum directions, loving and hating my Chinese year. I ride my bike to the market, and a man wearing a red arm band chides me, grinning, pointing out that I've parked too close to some white line. Street traffic is a chaos, any safety rule seems randomly ignored, and yet the lines of parking spaces count. Then the toothless friendly women in the market soothe my anger. And later in some local restaurant with dingy floors but hand-wiped tables, I say to Peggy, this place is really clean, and she agrees, laughing, watching our old standards shift on Chinese sands. The certain truth is this—that every time I've said I hate this country, something has surprised me into love, some dim-lit street with the hush of cyclists peddling home, some water buffalo beside the window of a passing train.

Like my Chinese friends, I start to make my explanations in parables, a metaphor for what defies pinning down. I choose the story of the emperor who went to Yangzhou, had such good luck fishing there that he gave the town a gift of great wealth. His luck was really swimmers, hiding underwater, putting fish on his hook. An old version of the back-door machinations of China, but also of the mysterious way that good things come so unexpectedly here.

And still I think that everything I tell you could be wrong somehow, or right but slightly crooked, or the opposite tomorrow. The names glow once inside my hands and wing off into darkness. Naming the truth of China is like counting the stone-carved lions on Lougouqiao, the long bridge in Beijing that tourist books name after Marco Polo because he so admired it. The legend says it's impossible to count the lions, and if by chance someone did get the total right once, they'd disappear.

Sibyl James earned a Ph.D. in English Literature from SUNY (Buffalo) and is currently a Fulbright Professor at the University of Tunis (Tunisia). Her books include *The White Junk of Love, Again* (CALYX Books, 1986) and *Vallarta Street* (Laughing Dog Press, 1988). She is the recipient of numerous awards for her writing, including the first Creative Writing Fellowship from the Artist's Trust (Seattle, WA), the Washington Poet's Association William Stafford Award, and the Pacific Northwest Writers Association Award. Her work has been published widely in more than 100 literary journals, including *CALYX* and *The American Voice*. She has also taught English at the University of Guadalajara (Mexico), the Shanghai Institute of Foreign Trade (People's Republic of China), Highline Community College (Seattle, WA), and the University of Washington (Seattle).

The text of this book is composed in Palatino.
Typeset by ImPrint Services, Corvallis, Oregon.